THE GREAT
WIZARD WARS

THE GREAT WIZARD WARS

CHRISTINA CLARRY

Matador
9 Priory Business Park,
Wistow Road, Kibworth Beauchamp,
Leicestershire, LE8 0RX
Tel: 0116 279 2299
Email: books@troubador.co.uk
Web: www.troubador.co.uk/matador
Twitter: @matadorbooks

ISBN 978 1785898 358

British Library Cataloguing in Publication Data.
A catalogue record for this book is available from the British Library.

Printed and bound in the UK by TJ International, Padstow, Cornwall
Typeset in 12pt Book Antiqua by Troubador Publishing Ltd, Leicester, UK

Matador is an imprint of Troubador Publishing Ltd

For my children and their children who have never ceased to inspire me with their magical imaginations and endless thirst for knowledge. Without them, this book would never have been written.

PROLOGUE

In the far distant past, two mighty forces clashed in the first Great Wizard War. It was a battle of good against evil. A Golden Army against a Dark Army!

Golden Wizards and Witches riding dragons were an awesome sight as they flew into battle in their uniform of golden robes, led by the Great Warrior Wizard, Lanzor.

They faced the evil Dark Warlord, Mortor, and his army of Deadly Wizards and Witches. This fearsome army, dressed in black, swooped through the skies on enslaved warhorses.

Both sides engaged in armed combat as well as casting spells against each other. The Dark Army constantly attacked first and the Golden Army retaliated valiantly.

Despite the Dark Army suffering heavier

losses, Mortor stubbornly continued the onslaught. Their evil numbers dwindled. Finally, the Dark Warlord was slain and the Dark Army surrendered. Their lives were spared on condition they signed a truce. The terms of the truce were that war was never to be waged again, and that Lanzor should take charge of the bodies of all who had fallen in battle. He would have the bodies hidden and guarded. For a time would come when spells powerful enough to bring them all back to life would be found. Reluctantly, the Dark Army agreed to these terms. Both armies were disbanded.

The surviving good wizards and witches stayed together and lived peacefully. On the other hand, the evil wizards and witches simply vanished into dark places, living alone or in small groups, deep in woods and forests. Being evil, they found it impossible to live together in a community. Their nature was to argue and fight.

Meanwhile, dragons were rarely seen after the Great Wizard War. The survivors found deserted islands to live on. In the ensuing years their numbers built up again. They have remained on their islands enjoying undisturbed lives.

The warhorses, too, were battle weary. They returned to their remote mountains and sheltered in caves to avoid being seen and captured for evil purposes.

The truce was to last for many centuries... until an evil descendant of Mortor appeared...

A MAGIC VILLAGE

It was the last day of term in Obscura's School of Magic. Rows of young wizards and witches were buzzing with excitement. Classes had been combined for the last lesson and friends were able to sit next to each other in the large assembly room. They were waiting for their teacher, Bella, to enter in her usual dramatic fashion. She was a favourite of theirs. Never boring! She taught Drama and History and turned what could be incredibly dull history lessons into action-packed, spectacular journeys into the past!

A door crashed open and in rushed a small witch in a dark green robe with bright red hair flying behind her. She stopped abruptly in front of the sea of faces and taking a deep breath slowly blew it out again. The room fell silent and the class waited in anticipation. Bella loved to command the centre stage.

'Good afternoon, everyone.'

'Good afternoon, Bella,' they all chorused.

Only first names were used here.

'Today, we will discuss our magic village, Obscura,' Bella announced. She swept both hands through the air and tilted her head back, allowing her long curls to untangle down her back. She knew how to hold every eye in the room.

There was a low groan. The class had doubts that even Bella could make this an exciting topic. Some chatter could be heard from the back.

'Will you PAY ATTENTION!' Bella raised her voice. 'I know you think Obscura is BORING! But that is only because you live here. If you lived in an ordinary old English village then you really would be bored to death! You need to understand *why* and *how* Obscura is unique.' She pretended to be at her wits end. 'Children of today would drive me out of teaching if this was an ordinary school!'

This caught their interest. She spun around and glared at them. Bella realised that the class loved to see her in full battle mode. THAT made history exciting! She was a FIERY witch when her blood boiled! They all smiled at her, which seemed to infuriate her more. She was a brilliant actress. Bella strode dramatically across the floor, stopped in front of a boy and pointed straight at him!

'Stand up and tell me in less than one minute when and why Obscura was built? And speak up! The whole class would like to know as well.'

Danny stood up. He was tall for his age with

jet-black, close-cropped hair and intensely dark eyes. Everyone was expectant. This was going to be good. Danny had a sense of humour and enjoyed bating Bella. He would show them how boring this topic was! He tilted his head and adjusted imaginary spectacles over his nose in the same manner that old Perkin, the science wizard, used.

'Err … oomph!' he cleared his throat and paused, while peering at his audience. The whole class giggled.

Bella spluttered … 'That's ten seconds gone!'

Danny was not to be rushed. 'Err … oomph,' he repeated, with another pause that was intended to bore you to death. 'Obscura was built in the Middle Ages by the descendants of good wizards and witches, who had survived the Great Wizard War. They wanted a safe, secret place, hidden from evil wizards and witches. It was also vital to protect their village from ordinary people because of the Witch Hunts taking place at that time. They made Obscura appear dull and *boring*. There were no inns or taverns. So, any passing travellers moved on. There was nothing of interest and nowhere to stay. Err … oomph.'

Danny lifted his arm and pretended to peer at his wristwatch, then nodded his head. His minute was up. The class applauded Danny, mainly for his imitation of old Perkin. He bowed to his audience. They all clapped harder. Danny bowed again and sat down.

Ginny, the girl sitting next to Danny, jabbed him in ribs and said in a loud stage whisper that everyone could hear, 'Very good, and *very* boring, Perkin!'

The class burst out laughing! Ginny was full of fun and she and Danny were great friends.

Bella brought her hands together and drummed her fingers against each other. She pretended to be annoyed but she was enjoying the mix of history with drama.

There was a hush. Bella was about to pounce on someone else. She pointed her finger straight at Ginny. 'Your chance to bore us now! Stand up and tell us why we try to keep Obscura hidden from evil wizards and witches?'

Ginny stood up. She was Danny's age and almost as tall as him. Her head was covered in brown curls. She had an infectious, playful smile on her face. No one knew that Ginny had spent the week practicing her imitation of Bella! She stood up and swept around to face the class, tossing her head back. She took a deep breath and slowly exhaled. The whole class tried desperately to suppress their laughter. But when they saw Bella's expression, the laughter erupted!

Bella pouted and put her hands on her hips. Her eyes flashed at the class. 'We are waiting with bated breath to hear you, Ginny!' She did her best to sound menacing but was secretly amused.

Ginny rubbed her hands together. She intended to give a fiery performance! Striding across the front of the room, she spoke loudly and confidently.

'Where do I start?' Ginny tossed her head back and glared at the class with her hands on her hips. The class giggled. Ginny glowered at them.

'To begin with, evil wizards and witches are incredibly *stupid!* They fight and squabble *all* the time. They can't control their evil nature. Like ... in the Great Wizard War ... they just kept on attacking our army who had dragons to fight on. Any idiot could see they didn't have a chance of winning! But they kept on trying ... and lost. The truce they agreed to says they must never form another army to attack us, but that wouldn't stop them causing all sorts of other trouble. They cause havoc wherever they are!'

The class stamped their feet and clapped. This was strong stuff! Bella suppressed a smile and glowered at Ginny.

Ginny glowered back. Then, raising her voice, she continued in an angry tone. 'Those twits are dumb and stuck in the Dark Ages because they are incapable of learning anything new. Or learning anything at all! But worst of all, they are cowardly and underhand. They take hostages and use torture!' It was difficult to tell if Ginny was acting now. She looked genuinely outraged.

Taking a deep breath, she paused and inclined her head. Then, she spun around and sat down.

Ginny had made quite an impact. They all held their breath waiting for Bella's reaction. Bella looked directly at Ginny, nodded her head slowly and clapped. The class joined in.

Bella found that act hard to follow. She simply tossed her head back and eyed the group of friends sitting together who were best known as, "The Feisty Four". An apt nickname, she thought. Danny and Ginny were the older two. Danny's brother, Josh, was sitting next to him and grinning wickedly. Ginny's sister, Katy, looked slightly embarrassed to be at the centre of attention.

Bella locked eyes with Josh. 'Your turn, young man! Come to the front and tell us about Obscura School and how it differs from the ordinary schools of today. In one minute.'

Josh stood up with a twinkle in his dark brown eyes. He was agile for his age and very energetic and mischievous but in a fun way. Scratching his head through his dark blonde hair, he thought for a second or two.

'From the outside our school looks like other small village schools, but it is huge inside! We have an awesome sports hall and swimming pool hidden underground. Our library doesn't have ordinary reading books. It has books we experience! We have intelligent androids that cook our meals and clean the school. Our lessons are fun. Classes are combined, like this one, for History or Drama.' Josh paused and grinned widely, 'But I don't know which lesson this is meant to be!'

Several voices shouted in glee, 'WE DON'T KNOW EITHER!'

Josh continued with enthusiasm. 'We learn how to make magic potions and how to cast spells. And we have crazy teachers like ...'

The class finished Josh's sentence. 'QUIRKOR!' they all shouted!

'THANK YOU, Josh!' Bella interrupted above the laughter. 'Your minute is up.' Bella should have known from the twinkle in Josh's eye that he would have the last laugh. But she had to admit that Quirkor was as mad as a hatter! He was always testing and casting new spells that sometimes went horribly wrong. Quirkor was in charge of the Potions and Spells class. He had blown the roof off the school last year! Before pupils dare to go into his class, they put protection spells on themselves!

Bella threw up both hands until the class quietened down. Then she turned the spotlight on Katy, who was next to Josh. She was the quietest and most thoughtful of the Feisty Four. The other three were protective of her. She looked like a fragile doll with long smooth black hair. 'I can't leave you out, Katy. We would value your opinion as one of the Feisty Four! Please step up here.'

Katy blushed as she stood up. She swallowed nervously.

Ginny whispered encouragingly. 'It's OK, Sis. We're here for you!'

Bella stroked her chin, thoughtfully. She needed to end the lesson on a serious note and Katy could do this. 'Katy, tell us about the extraordinary houses in Obscura and why ordinary people never move here to live?'

Katy took a shaky breath and lifted her head. 'Our houses may look normal to ordinary people on the outside but they are amazing inside. We cast spells to turn our rooms into places we enjoy. When a spell wears off, we can change them again. A dining room can be small and cosy one day and a banquet hall the next! The space inside can be stretched. We never need to move to a new house. Houses in our village are never sold. So an outsider would never see a "FOR SALE" sign or find a house to buy here.'

Katy was feeling more confident as she continued. 'We rarely see strangers as no roads lead here, just old dirt tracks. No delivery lorries or postal vans come from other towns because we grow or make everything we need. Outsiders have never heard of Obscura.'

'Well said, Katy.' Bella swept her eyes over the class. She could see they were distracted by something behind her. There was a loud, guttural purr. A huge black and white cat had wandered in. It was Merlin, who spent much of his time in the school. Everyone was fond of Merlin. And Merlin was fond of everyone. He was that sort of cat.

Merlin's sixth sense told him that it was the end of term. He had come into the last lesson to choose someone to stay with during the holidays. Merlin strutted past Bella and rubbed himself against Katy. Then he jumped onto Ginny's lap. He decided he would share his feline love with these two girls.

Bella knew she had lost everyone's attention. 'This is a short session. So, I will conclude it now by reminding you that Obscura must remain looking like a boring old village from the outside. Yet it is a secretive and wonderful place to live in. Today, ordinary people don't believe wizards and witches exist. We must maintain that impression if we wish to be left in peace. Your homework for the holiday is an essay, *"Obscura Village, as seen by outsiders and how we see it!"* Describe any encounters you or your families have had with ordinary people. The best essays will be read out next term.'

There was a chorus of moans. Boring homework!

Bella attempted to glare sternly at them. Then she swirled around and gave them all a huge smile. 'Enjoy your holiday!'

The class rose as Bella swept out of the room. They all followed closely behind.

The Feisty Four grinned at each other as

they walked out. They were inseparable in school. During holidays, they always spent time together.

Ginny turned to Danny and Josh. 'We'll see you at my birthday party next week.'

'Can't wait to see the surprise you have in store for us all,' Danny replied.

'Dad and Wizzo worked hard to have it ready in time,' Katy told them.

'I bet it'll be amazing if Wizzo was involved!' Josh sounded thrilled.

After saying goodbye outside the school gates, the girls went one way with Merlin bounding after them, while the boys headed in the opposite direction to their home.

Danny and Josh lived on the edge of the village. Their house looked out onto meadows with thickets in the distance. The land belonged to all the villagers and it was left to grow wild. It provided a natural zone between the village and the outside world.

There was no street sign to be seen but all the villagers called this Owl Lane for it was popular with these birds. The wild fields were their hunting grounds at night.

As the boys approached their gate, they spotted their dad, Felix, in the garden and waved. He was busy selecting herbs for his potions, which the villagers rated highly for curing ailments.

They looked critically at their house with new

eyes. It was indeed very ordinary on the outside. On entering, they found their mother, Fabia, in the kitchen flipping through a witch's recipe book. She was deciding which special cake she would make for Ginny's birthday. Fabia was plump and jolly and always smelt of vanilla and spice.

'Did you have a good day at school?' she asked with a wide smile. 'I hope you don't have too much homework for the holidays.'

'School was OK, Mom,' Danny replied. 'But Bella set an essay on how our village looks through an ordinary person's eyes and how we see it.'

'Even the younger ones have to do it,' Josh groaned. 'It'll take me ages!'

Fabia crossed the room and put her arms around their shoulders. 'Your dad and I can help you with that.'

Felix came into the kitchen. He looked like a healthy farmer with his weathered tan. He had a hearty attitude. 'Hello, boys!' he said cheerfully. 'I caught what you said about homework. We'll certainly help you with that. When you go to bed, your mom and I will cast a memory spell on you both while you sleep. It will bring back everything you know about Obscura.'

'Awesome, Dad! Josh and I have never had one of those spells cast on us before,' Danny said. 'I think I'll write the essay tomorrow and get it over with.'

Josh looked less enthusiastic. Although he

knew the spell would be fun, the essay would take him a long time.

Fabia noticed Josh's silence. 'Don't worry about lost time, Josh. We'll also cast a spell to make your pens write faster!'

Josh grinned in delight. 'Thanks, Mom!'

After Danny and Josh fell sleep that night, Felix and Fabia quietly took out their wands and waved them over each boy as they chanted, 'Somnia de Obscura.'

Soon the boys' dreams were a fascinating web of their memories and experiences of their magical village …

In their first dream they were entering The Olde Bookshop on the village High Street. This was no ordinary bookshop with books sitting on shelves. The first thing they saw was a wise old wizard sitting in front of a warm, welcoming fire. Hovering all over the large room were books on spells and every topic imaginable.

The old wizard smiled at them both and said, 'Welcome back, boys. Tell me which book you want to experience today.'

'Please can we have one about dinosaurs in the Cretaceous period,' Josh replied. 'It's for a school project.'

The old wizard nodded and pointed his wand at a large volume at the far end of the room. It floated slowly towards them and grew into the size of a door. The book opened.

'Step inside boys. Come out when you are finished. If you like the book, you can take it home.'

Danny and Josh stepped into the book and straight into a scene from millions of years ago. There was lush, green vegetation everywhere. Their mouths fell open as they stopped in front of 3D images of two dinosaurs. The book told them, 'In front of you is an Ankylosaurus carefully walking around a Triceratops. Both were plant eaters and not interested in fighting each other. To protect itself from carnivorous flesh-eating dinosaurs, the Ankylosaurus had armoured plates over its body and a massive tail club, while the Triceratops would use the three horns on its head if attacked.'

'If I was a hungry dinosaur, I wouldn't fancy fighting one of those,' whispered Josh.

'Wow! It's big … it must be nine metres long,' exclaimed Danny as he stared at the Triceratops while it sauntered by them.

There was a swamp ahead and they saw a Diplodocus wading through the water to the edge where some conifers were growing. With its long neck, it easily reached into the trees and began to strip off large mouthfuls of foliage with its blunt teeth.

The book informed them, 'That dinosaur is over twenty metres long and weighs nearly twenty tons.'

'No wonder it likes to be in water,' Josh said

in wonder. 'I'd want to take the weight off my feet if I was a Diplodocus!'

'You'll certainly remember facts if you keep imagining yourself to be a dinosaur, Josh,' Danny said jokingly.

Josh turned to his brother and uttered a ferocious growl. 'I'm a T-Rex and I'm hungry!' He stomped on the ground and let out another fierce growl.

Suddenly the boys jumped with fright as a large head rose up from amongst the giant ferns and horsetails growing nearby. It opened its mouth to display massive teeth and roared back!

'It's a T-Rex!' both boys yelled in unison as the deadly dinosaur hurtled towards them through the undergrowth.

Danny grabbed Josh's arm. 'Don't worry, it's only 3D. Remember!' Danny tried to sound reassuring.

Both boys stood shock still as the mighty beast pounded towards them. The ground shook! It surged past them and leapt onto the Ankylosaurus! A mighty battle ensued while the boys watched transfixed. Finally, the T-Rex flipped the Ankylosaurus onto its back where it lay helpless with its unprotected belly exposed.

This book was incredibly exciting and more than the boys could have hoped for. When they finally stepped out of the magical book, they told the old wizard that they definitely wanted it.

'Mmm, I thought so,' the old wizard mused

while he brought the book down to its original size. 'As usual, when you want to go in again, just tap the book with one of your wands.'

When they left, the boys grinned at the books in the shop window. In case an ordinary person passed by, there were some boring volumes on display. Nobody would want to read *One Week in the Life of a Snail* and rush inside to buy it!

Their next dream took them into another favourite place, Ye Olde Farrier's Stables, on the outskirts of the village. Outsiders could only see a blacksmith's yard behind the gates, but wizards and witches could enter an underground manufacturing plant via a secret door in the stables! Anything that could be imagined was made here, from robots to electric bikes. In charge of the whole complex was a brilliant wizard named Wizzo. This huge wizard sat in his office surrounded by oversized computer screens.

The Feisty Four had recently gone there to choose hoverboards. This was the latest craze. Everyone in school wanted one. Broomsticks were so out of fashion! Wizzo listened carefully to their wishes. Then turning to his keyboard, which was an assortment of symbols, he tapped away with his fingers flying. 3D models of hoverboards projected out of the screens. Danny and Josh had great fun choosing two designed for speed. Ginny and Katy opted for models that they could quickly manoeuvre in tag games.

Spells could have been cast by any of them to create hoverboards, but spells wear off! Every spell has a limited life. Some last for years but others last just a few minutes. New spells were unpredictable … it would be nasty if their hoverboards disappeared from under them when going at top speed! Wizzo's products were safe and guaranteed to last as he used high-tech methods and materials.

Danny and Josh's dreams jumped to the day they were walking down the High Street and saw two hikers, who must have accidentally stumbled across their village. They were a young couple with rucksacks on their backs. Just before the hikers noticed Danny and Josh, their wizards' robes magically changed into ordinary clothes! Just as they were supposed to …

When the boys had collected their new robes from Splendora's Clothes Shoppe, Splendora had asked them what clothes they would like their robes to turn into, should they meet outsiders. They had both chosen jeans and t-shirts. The friendly witch had waved her wand over their robes and chanted, 'Mutationis!' The robes had instantly transformed into ordinary clothes. 'Try them on, boys. Must make sure they're the right size. Don't want them falling off you in public,' she laughed. Both boys had reddened at the thought and hurried into the changing rooms to check they fitted.

... and now they needed them! Danny and Josh looked at each other. Unconsciously, they had both checked their jeans weren't falling off. They smiled ruefully and continued to walk down the street.

The young couple appeared to be interested in the shops. They tried to enter one but there was a sign, CLOSED FOR THE DAY, on the door. The door of the next shop was also locked with another identical notice, CLOSED FOR THE DAY. They looked puzzled when they found the third shop was shut as well.

By now, Danny and Josh were about to walk past them when the man asked, 'Why are all the shops closed? Where is everybody?'

The villagers had a standard reply to these questions. With the most serious look he could muster, Danny replied, 'They will all be going to a funeral.'

This was not really a lie. One day, everyone *would* be going to a funeral!

'Oh, I'm so sorry to hear that!' exclaimed the woman.

The man had a further question or two to ask. 'Before you go boys, can you tell us where we are? We can't find this location on our map. And we couldn't see any signposts leading here.'

'Maybe the map is out of date,' Josh suggested as innocently as he could.

Before the man could say anything further, Danny turned and looked meaningfully at Josh.

'We have to hurry home. We're late for lunch,' he said.

The boys waved goodbye and left the hikers looking puzzled and disappointed to find nothing of interest. As the hikers walked away, the shop doors unlocked and the signs changed to read, OPEN.

As soon as the boys turned a corner, their wizards' robes materialised.

'We should follow them and make sure they leave the village,' Danny said in a low voice.

'Let's cast invisibility spells,' Josh whispered. They pulled out their wands and pointing them at each other, quietly chanted, 'Invisibilia!'

The boys retraced their steps and quietly followed the hikers.

On the outskirts of the village, the couple were frustrated by the lack of directions. 'There isn't even a decent road to follow. How can anyone find this place?' muttered the man in annoyance.

'Perhaps it doesn't want to be found,' the woman replied.

'Just as well, there's nothing to do here. Nothing!' he said in disgust. 'Let's go!'

Danny and Josh watched them disappear down one of the dirt tracks.

'Geesh!' Danny exclaimed. 'Obscura really *is* the most boring place on earth to outsiders! If only they knew …'

Both boys laughed. Then they reversed

their invisibility spells and went home. When they sat down to lunch with their parents, they described their meeting with the two hikers. Felix and Fabia listened with amusement.

'We rarely see outsiders,' Felix had said. 'Hopefully, they will soon forget what appears to be a dull old village, like all the other accidental visitors.'

Fabia chuckled. 'I'm not so sure that rude couple in the car we came across last month will forget so easily!'

Felix roared with laughter at the memory. 'They said their Sat Nav and mobile phones were behaving oddly. But we know that was due to Wizzo's scrambling signals hiding the village. The man was very irate! He told us that they had driven around the village looking for a way in but there were NO ENTRY signs everywhere. When they asked us where the nearest car park was, I said, "Try Foxton Village." I thought the man would blow up! He drove off in a cloud of dust muttering something about a village full of halfwits!'

Everyone had joined in the laughter, secure in the thought that Obscura was safe for wizards and witches like them.

The boys continued dreaming through the night … this was a magical place to live in.

EVIL ARRIVES

As the whole family slept peacefully, they were completely unaware that a new neighbour had arrived during the night!

A heavy silence descended as a severe, angry-looking wizard moved into the empty house next door. He had searched for a secluded house on the furthest edge of the village and the end house on Owl Lane suited his plans perfectly.

His appearance was foreboding and sombre. He arrived at midnight, and his black robe and wizard's hat made it difficult to see him in the shadows. His dark grey hair and long beard were barely visible. Then the blackest, piercing eyes flashed in the dark. Only the wildlife in the garden saw him arrive. As the temperature plummeted, evil seemed to fill the air. The owls flew away. Hedgehogs scurried next door, and tiny shrews decided that the meadows opposite would be safer.

When dawn broke, the last of the birds flew

away and even the bees left. The frogs and toads from the garden pond were just leaving to find another watery home when the grim wizard came out and immediately barred their way!

'Oh no, you don't! I have many uses for you slimy lot! Spells! Frogs on toast! Which reminds me … it's breakfast time.'

The horrified amphibians fled back to the pond, dived in and hid amongst the pondweed at the bottom. He cackled hideously. It was the most evil laugh imaginable.

'Now to stop anyone or anything entering.' Pulling out his wand, he swept it along the boundaries of the garden and chanted, 'Muros de spinis!' Thick high walls of brambles appeared where a low fence had been. Long dagger-like thorns sprouted and interlocked, making the walls look menacing.

The wizard then pointed his wand upwards and chanted, 'Malum obice in caelum!' An ominous aura began to form over the house and garden. It looked like a dome of grey radiation. 'That will kill anything uninvited that tries to fly through it!' he muttered with malice.

The family next door had risen early as well. They were entering the kitchen for breakfast when Danny looked through the window and gasped, 'Something weird is happening next door!'

The other three turned to look in the same direction. There was a stunned silence.

'Look at that wall of brambles! It wasn't there yesterday!' Josh said in surprise.

'And that is some sort of dark aura over the house,' whispered Fabia, as a cold shiver ran down her spine.

'We appear to have a new neighbour. But he doesn't appear to be welcoming. In fact, he seems to want to keep everyone out … or something in …' Felix said in a low voice. 'I will try to find out who it is after breakfast.'

While the family sat down to eat, their unexpected neighbour made changes to his house. He created a large underground vaulted dungeon where he intended to spend most of the daytime. He wasn't interested in the other rooms. He didn't need much sleep … there were far better things to do at night! And anyone coming here would not be sleeping!

The new inhabitant was making sure no one uninvited was welcome there. The only way anyone would learn his name, would be from the sign he hung outside his gate. It read, PRIVATE! KEEP OUT! and CRYPTOR was written below the warning.

After breakfast, Felix went next door. But he could only get as far as the gate. The aura stopped above it, but it was locked and chained. He was deeply worried when he read the sign. Returning to his house, he addressed the family. 'Our new neighbour is called Cryptor. That is the name displayed on a sign outside his house, which warns you not to enter! There is no one in the village by that name today. There is a possibility that he may be one of our good wizards, who left many years ago to tend the fallen dragons in Fire Mountain and has now returned. As you know from history, the brave dragons that fell in the Great Wizard War lie in Fire Mountain. Years of living in solitude, in the mountain caves, may have made a wizard returning here want to continue living a private life. We will leave him alone until we find out more about him.'

Strange things began to happen. Cryptor would disappear at night and return at dawn. While he was out during the night, towns were flooded or earthquakes rocked whole cities. The news reports the following morning were bad.

During the day, Cryptor remained inside his house and never had visitors. Dark clouds gathered above his house and the grey aura appeared to be strengthening over it. The cold temperature surrounding Cryptor's house began to seep down Owl Lane.

Felix and Fabia began to suspect the worst! Could Cryptor be an evil wizard? But why would one come to their village when they hated living in communities? All evil wizards were bound by the truce agreed by their ancestors to keep peace. And why were terrible things happening when he was out at night?

'We must keep an eye on Cryptor. I suspect he has evil plans in mind,' whispered Felix so he would not worry the boys.

'Yes, I can sense evil coming from there, too. Cryptor is dangerous,' agreed Fabia. 'We will need to be wary and start casting spells to stop his evil acts whenever he goes out.'

Meanwhile, next door, one of the most evil descendants of the Deadly Wizards was plotting to wipe out the whole village! He had moved there to observe the inhabitants and work out their weaknesses. Cryptor was spying on the village! He had chosen the empty house on Owl Lane as the perfect base to operate from.

His nightly trips of destruction were to attract the attention of all the other evil descendants of the Deadly Wizards and Witches. They would recognise the evil magic behind the damage he was causing and come out, after centuries of hiding, to meet him. Cryptor then greeted them like long lost friends and told them the reason for seeking them out. He delivered a warmongering speech every time!

'My plan is to build a new Dark Army of Deadly Wizards and Witches. A stronger one than our ancestors had during the Great Wizard War! For too long, we have been held back by the truce that was signed after the Dark Warlord was slain in battle. We know he lies out there somewhere waiting for us to bring him and our fallen ancestors back into the world. I suspect their bodies have been hidden near a village called Obscura and is heavily guarded by the descendants of the Golden Wizards and Witches living there. This village is their stronghold. I have finally found it after many long years of searching.'

Cryptor would pause dramatically while this sank in and then would deliver his plan. 'It is time for us to rise up again! When our new army has the numbers needed, we will attack secretly and swiftly before they suspect anything and destroy them all. We must search for a spell to bring the Dark Warlord and our ancestors to life! Then together we will begin our worldwide attacks. We will rule the world and spare no one who stands in our way! I will summon you all to join me in Obscura before the week is out. By then, I will have the numbers required for our new Dark Army. We will launch the surprise attack at night. WILL YOU JOIN ME IN THIS NEW WAR?' Cryptor cried as he pumped the air with his clenched fist! 'From today we will be known as the Deadly Wizards and Witches of the new Dark Army!'

Every single one of them shouted, 'YES!' They had been waiting a long, long time to fight another war …

Only two more nights of destruction were needed by Cryptor to complete his army!
On his latest trip, Cryptor aimed to flood

the whole coast of east England. As usual, the Deadly Wizard set off during the night. He shunned modern day transport. Cryptor was stuck in the Dark Ages and preferred to call up magical creatures to carry him. In his arrogance, he thought he looked far more imposing mounted on these mythical animals. For once, he was right!

Cryptor decided to summon Chakora, a giant lunar bird, to fly him to the coast. Pointing his wand to the moon he chanted 'Luna avis!'

A huge silver bird came gliding down the moonbeams and through a hole in Cryptor's aura that he had opened up for it. It landed gracefully and eyed Cryptor with intense suspicion. Chakora sensed Cryptor was evil but his spell was impossible to overcome.

'Don't look at me like that you scrawny louse bag! Or I'll give you the evil eye! Come here!' he growled.

Closing its eyes in an effort to avoid Cryptor's threat, the big bird hopped towards Cryptor and misjudging the distance, knocked him clean off his feet.

'YOU STUPID, IDIOTIC, CRAZY PILE OF USELESS FEATHERS! OPEN YOUR EYES OR I'LL ROAST YOU FOR DINNER!' Cryptor screeched at the top of his voice!

He leapt up in fury, threw a chain around the lunar bird's neck and hauled himself onto its back, carelessly dislodging some feathers.

'Head east as fast as the wind and don't stop until we reach the coast!' he ordered.

Chakora rose into the air and through the hole in the aura with elegant sweeps of its wings. As it hovered above Cryptor's house, some of its loose feathers fell onto the aura. Sparks flashed and the feathers were instantly incinerated! Only puffs of smoke remained. In complete terror, Chakora sped east as fast as its wings could go.

Cryptor had not noticed Felix and Fabia pointing their wands at him and chanting, 'Prohibere malus magicus!' as he disappeared into the distance!

Within two hours, the sea came into sight. It looked calm with the moon reflecting on gently rippling waves.

Cryptor cackled gruesomely as he imagined the chaos he was about to cause. He intended to cast a spell that would create a huge tidal surge. Gigantic waves would sweep across the low-lying land and flood every town and city in the vicinity!

As they flew over the coastline, Cryptor pointed his wand and shouted, 'Aqua ubique!' The Deadly Wizard waited in anticipation for massive waves to swamp the land. All the coastal homes would soon be flooded. He would enjoy watching people climbing onto their rooftops as their cars floated away in raging torrents below them!

Cryptor expected that many evil wizards and witches, witnessing this dark magic, would come out to seek him. Perhaps enough to complete his army!

But something was wrong! He looked at the sea. Nothing had happened! Just a few waves rippled gently onto the shore. He pointed his wand and tried again.

'AQUA UBIQUE!' he screamed with all his might.

Absolutely nothing happened. Waves continued to gently caress the shore in the moonlight. Cryptor was now demented with rage! He knew exactly who was to blame. Only a good spell could have neutralised his evil one. Cryptor loathed good wizards and witches with all his black heart. They were the only ones who could stand in his way. And they had been watching him recently.

'I'll teach those interfering cretins next door a lesson they'll never forget!' he vowed to himself through gritted teeth. With a face like thunder and in a foul and filthy mood, the Deadly Wizard spun the lunar bird around and ordered it to return to Obscura. He needed to deal with those good-for-nothing neighbours. He would make them suffer. Suffer in the worst way imaginable!

The sound of Cryptor returning woke the boys. They saw the evil wizard just before he entered his house as they peered out of their windows. Moonlight lit up his grim, hostile face as he turned towards them and scowled. Then he was gone.

Icy, cold fingers ran down their spines.

CRYPTOR'S SNAKE

Cryptor's first monstrous thought when he got back was to kill everyone next door! But before his fury got the better of him, he realised that killing them now would alert the whole village before he had his army in place.

Instead, he decided he would conjure up the strongest evil spell to stop Felix, Fabia and their two wizard brats from interfering for as long as possible. It would have to be a much more powerful spell than the ones they cast. And the one Cryptor intended to use would take away all their magic ability! He would need to acquire some of the most potent ingredients in the world for this spell. But these ingredients were rare and dangerous to find.

The Deadly Wizard decided to leave on his search for these as soon as possible. A lunar bird was no use for a trip that would take days. It would not fly in daylight.

For this trip, he would use one of the animals

that had been forced to serve the Dark Army centuries ago. A warhorse! Cryptor recalled how powerfully they were built. During battle, they had worn heavy suits of armour, as they had to fight dragons. With flowing red manes and tails and a pair of horns on their heads, they were a fearsome sight. Their long wings of swords were their most terrifying feature. These were as sharp as razors. They were deadly weapons in combat!

'Yes! A warhorse is just what I need for this search. There is a great distance to travel to find the creature that will supply my first powerful ingredient,' Cryptor mused to himself.

The Deadly Wizard pointed his wand to the sky and chanted, 'Bellum Equus!' Cryptor waited patiently until a heavily built warhorse appeared on the horizon. Its long swords flashed in the first shafts of sunrise as it approached and circled overhead. Cryptor opened a hole in the evil aura over his house and the magnificent animal swooped down and landed in front of him. It pawed the ground with its huge hooves, impatient to be gone.

Cryptor snarled at the warhorse, 'I warn you now, if you put a foot wrong, it will be the end of you!'

There had never been an easy relationship between the Deadly Wizards and warhorses. Much cruelty and evil magic had been used to enslave these wild creatures. In truth, warhorses hated the Deadly Wizards but feared them more. And so, they had grudgingly become their war steeds.

Cryptor lashed a heavy chain around the warhorse's neck and hauled himself onto its back avoiding the swords. The creature snorted in anger.

'STEADY NOW, YOU BRUTE!' Cryptor yelled and gritted his teeth as the heavy horse reared up. 'Go south, and be quick about it, if you value your life!'

The warhorse leapt up with its huge swords cutting through the air. They rose through the hole in the evil aura on the first long journey Cryptor had planned.

Felix, Fabia, and the boys were still asleep when Cryptor left. If they had seen the warhorse, it would have been the final proof that Cryptor was evil. Good wizards and witches had never used warhorses, for they deserved to be free after being abused by the Dark Army.

In the morning, they wondered where Cryptor had gone but were relieved at the same time. All was peaceful, once more. And the air felt warmer again.

Meanwhile, Cryptor was travelling south. He kept the warhorse tracking the French coast, and just as they were about to enter Spain, gale force westerly winds began to slow the warhorse down and blow them off course. Cryptor could see that the warhorse was too tired to go any further and directed it to land on one of the last remaining glaciers in the Pyrenees Mountains.

He yelled at the warhorse above the howling gale, 'Cut an ice cave with your wings. We'll shelter there until this gale blows over!'

Cryptor was good at creating storms but he had never cast spells to stop them. Evil wizards did not do that.

Desperately weary, the warhorse used the last of its energy to carve out a shelter in the ice. Thankfully, it fell to its knees and lay down in exhaustion. The chains round it neck rattled against the icy floor.

Cryptor glared at it. 'Pathetic! You had better get used to this. There's much further to go, you useless piece of horsemeat!'

The warhorse was too tired to even raise its head, but its hatred for this vile wizard was building up inside.

Eventually, the storm abated during the night, and the next morning the warhorse managed to rise to its feet and drink some water from the melting glacier.

'Time to go,' Cryptor muttered as he climbed onto the warhorse. They flew south again over Spain and the Mediterranean Sea, heading for Africa. The cold air changed to searing heat as they approached the coastline.

Using thermal currents that rose from the scorching land, the warhorse soared from one to the next, trying to conserve its energy as they flew over North Africa and the arid deserts below them. After flying for the whole day, the deserts gave way to the jungles of West Africa. Finally, Cryptor saw the Congo River.

'Land here,' Cryptor directed, 'on the edge of that swamp. It's the exact spot for what I'm looking for.'

Gratefully, the exhausted warhorse landed. It was now half starved and desperately thirsty. There was wonderful green foliage to eat here and water in the swamp. As soon as Cryptor dismounted, it started to feed hungrily.

Cryptor eyed it with disdain. 'Eat while you can. You'll need it for the journey back. There will be a heavier load to carry!' He laughed.

The warhorse ignored Cryptor. But, out of the corner of its eye, it saw the evil wizard setting up a noose trap around the entrance to an opening in the ground. Something must live down there that the evil wizard wants badly, the warhorse realised.

Cryptor hid amongst the thick jungle ferns and creepers, holding the end of the noose, and waited. Darkness began to fall and the night noises of the jungle started. Huge bullfrogs from the swamp began their raucous chorus.

'A snake's favourite food. Might eat a couple, myself!' Cryptor cackled to himself.

He didn't have long to wait. An enormous serpent's head emerged from the hole. As quick as a flash, Cryptor hauled on the end of the rope and the noose tightened around the snake's neck. But the snake was incredibly strong and began to pull itself back down the hole with the rope still attached to it.

'Come here!' Cryptor yelled at the warhorse.

Rolling its eyes, the warhorse approached the evil wizard in trepidation. Cryptor reached up and tied the end of the noose to the chain around the warhorse's neck and ordered, 'Pull! Pull! Pull as hard as you can!' He slapped the creature hard and it reared back. Digging its hooves into the ground, it began to slowly pull the massive snake out of its hole.

It was everything an evil wizard could wish for. This snake was a cross between a rock python and a cobra. A massive venomous reptile! Magical properties abounded in its venom and skin. And this extraordinary snake would supply his spells with overwhelming power!

It was the result of a voodoo spell that had been cast by a West African witch. This witch was a descendant of the slaves who had been shipped to Haiti. She had returned home to Africa and created unique spells of her own. In one, she had combined the properties of the highly venomous cobra with the size and power of a python into one snake! As the spell had not created something out of nothing but had blended existing snakes, it did not fade with time! The witch had kept several of these snakes for her potions, but a couple of these giant reptiles had managed to escape into the jungle and had started to breed. It was a highly dangerous area. And Cryptor was right in the middle of it!

The warhorse stamped its hooves nervously as it saw the size of the reptile it had managed to drag out. The snake decided enough was enough. Seeing that the warhorse was responsible for its capture, the massive snake slithered towards it and raised its head up to attack. It opened its jaws wide and huge venomous fangs came up to strike the warhorse.

In total fright, the warhorse reared up and lashed out with its front hooves. One hoof caught the snake on the head and knocked it out! The warhorse stood there quivering in shock.

'Well, that saved me a lot of trouble,' Cryptor muttered ungratefully. He took a large roll of tape from his robe and proceeded to tape the snake's mouth shut.

'At least it can't bite when it wakes up. One drop of that venom is enough to kill ten of you!' he snorted. 'Now for a spell to keep it immobilised while we transport it back.' Cryptor took out his wand and pointed it at the snake. 'Somnum!' he chanted. 'That should keep it asleep!'

Turning to the warhorse, Cryptor snarled with a deadly undertone. 'You are going to fly with the snake over your back. Kneel down, while I drag it over you. Keep those swords out of the way!'

Much as the warhorse was tempted to use his swords against Cryptor and the captive snake, it knew evil would win. Shuddering, it dropped onto its hocks.

After hauling the sleeping snake over the warhorse, Cryptor climbed on behind it. The warhorse rose to its feet and with extra weight to carry, it needed all its power to lift off the ground and fly above the tree canopy. It was dreading the journey back.

Cryptor knew they would never make it back without help. He decided he would divert a strong jet stream, from ten miles up and hundreds of miles away, to come right down and sweep them back! He pointed his wand northwest into the sky and chanted, 'Movens ventus!'

The warhorse pricked its ears in alarm wondering what horror the evil wizard was concocting. For a couple of hours, the warhorse struggled to maintain height with its heavy load, until it heard the shriek of rushing wind. The jet stream had arrived in full force. Suddenly, they were scooped up and carried at an alarming speed over the jungle canopy. All the warhorse's flying skills were needed to keep its balance. The treetops bent and were ripped off as they passed overhead. As they sped over the desert, sand was sucked up and followed behind them in a huge dust storm.

They gained height and soon they were moving

at over two hundred miles an hour over the French coast. When the south coast of England came into sight, they left the jet stream and headed inland. Soon, they were descending over Cryptor's house. The Deadly Wizard opened a hole in the aura and the warhorse dropped through. It landed with a heavy thump on the ground looking totally dishevelled and windswept.

Without a word, Cryptor dismounted and dragged the snake off the warhorse. He pulled the deadly reptile across the garden and into his house. Slamming the door shut, Cryptor descended the steps to the dungeon and dropped the snake on the floor.

The warhorse shook itself, deeply relieved to finally be free of its terrible rider. With a shrill whinny, it darted through the hole in the aura before it closed. Then it headed as far away as it possibly could.

Down in the dungeon, Cryptor removed the tape from the snake's mouth while it was still sleeping. He wanted to extract as much venom from its fangs as possible. Cryptor had already set up the equipment necessary to do this before he set out on his journey. It was laid out on the dungeon table.

He reached for a membrane which he stretched and secured over a large glass vessel. Then Cryptor picked up the snake's head. It was heavy and he had to work quickly before the snake woke up. Prising the snake's mouth wide open to expose the long lethal fangs, Cryptor hooked them over the edge of the glass. The fangs pierced through the membrane and slowly venom began to seep from them and collected in a slimy pool at the bottom of the container. Cryptor milked every last drop of venom from the snake and then let the snake fall to the ground. Finally, he poured the venom into vials and secured the tops.

Satisfied with his handiwork, the Deadly Wizard looked at the snake. He needed snake skin for his spells, as well as venom. But that would have to wait until the snake moulted. The snake would have to literally grow out of its skin! The old skin would be shed and this is what Cryptor wanted.

The tail of the huge snake began to twitch. It was waking up. Slowly its eyes focused. It surveyed the cold dungeon walls and stone floor. It was freezing in here. Worst of all, in its sleep, it had seen its venom being drained ... as a snake sleeps with its eyes open! It had been robbed of its best defence. It glared at Cryptor.

'Don't you dare look at me like that, you vile serpent,' Cryptor spat at the snake. 'You are my prisoner and if you want to live ... you had better behave! You stay near the hearth, and I'll keep a low fire going to keep your blood warm enough for what I have in mind.' Cryptor did not want the snake going into a state of hibernation from the cold.

It was evident from the size and shape of the snake's stomach that it had eaten a huge meal recently and would be digesting the food and growing in size. Then it would moult.

'Saves me the trouble of feeding you,' Cryptor muttered to the snake. 'There will be no food for you here. I need you to be hungry for what I have planned. Really, really hungry when I release you in the village!'

The snake seemed to understand this threat and stared at Cryptor in pure disgust. If it had not been robbed of its venom, it would have launched itself at the evil wizard. Cryptor laughed in scorn at the powerless reptile.

The snake hissed loudly throughout the night, feeling angry and forlorn at its fate. It was furious about being held captive after the freedom of the jungle.

Next door, Felix and Fabia lay in bed and heard the snake.

'What on earth is going on?' whispered Fabia.

'It seems Cryptor has returned with a pet, but it doesn't sound very happy,' Felix said in a low voice.

Fabia did not reply.

They were extremely worried. Something ominous was in the air.

THE DRAGON CAPTURE

Cryptor knew speed was essential. Those neighbours could still ruin his plans if they suspected what he was up to.

He decided to set out again, before dawn, to capture the creature that would provide the most powerful ingredient of all for his evil spells. A dragon!

Dragons were now living on remote islands, and very few had been seen after the Great Wizard War. That war had started because of the same thing Cryptor was about to do. Capture and enslave a dragon!

Once, centuries ago, dragons had freely roamed the earth. They had lived peacefully among people until the clan of Deadly Wizards and Witches, lead by the Dark Warlord, had begun to trap and imprison them. Never before had spells been cast on dragons to overpower and capture them. They were completely unsuspecting. A

Dark Army was gathering which intended to use dragons to help them conquer the world. Terrible methods were used to torture and subdue the dragons. Young dragons were mercilessly taken as hostages.

The first dragons they captured were the small, friendly Bird Dragons. Then they trapped fiercer Fire Dragons and Sabre Dragons. Their plan was to round up all the remaining dragons. They especially wanted Chameleon Dragons. These were the fiercest of all dragons when aroused. Their evil army would then be unstoppable.

The Deadly Wizards and Witches ruthlessly caught whole families of dragons. They separated the young dragons from their parents. The captive adult dragons were heavily chained and kept hidden in a series of caves. The young dragons were forced into massive cages. These cages were then suspended over a river of molten lava that ran through the caves as their parents watched helplessly. They warned the dragons that if they tried to kill their captors when the spells on them wore off, the cages of young dragons would be dropped into the lava! Their cruelty knew no bounds!

But they had not reckoned on a dragon rebellion. One of the oldest and largest Fire Dragons named Zorgo managed to break free after melting the heavy chain that was keeping him shackled to the cave wall. It had taken every ounce of his fire breathing ability to do it. He was the only dragon there large enough to have sufficient firepower in his lungs for the task.

After the Deadly Wizards and Witches had left on their next dragon capture expedition, Zorgo had aimed his fiery breath at the links closest to the wall and pulled hard against the chain at the same time. A few of the links in the chain began to glow in the intense heat and slowly melt. After what had seemed an eternity, the chain had broken away from the wall and fallen to the floor with a clatter.

The other dragons had watched in alarm, fearful for the lives of the young dragons if the Deadly Wizards returned. Without hesitating, Zorgo had swooped across to the cages. With all the power he could muster in his powerful limbs, the Fire Dragon had gripped and bent the bars of each cage. The young dragons squeezed through and flew to safety … away from the molten lava.

Zorgo took command of the situation and communicated his intentions the way dragons do. By thought!

'There is no time to free you all. I will search for Lanzor, the great Warrior Wizard, and leader of the good wizards and witches and ask for help. We are close friends. He saved me from drowning when I was young. I trusted him to read my thoughts and I learnt his language.

I will explain that a Dark Army intends to wipe them out. When Lanzor hears we are being held in these caves and are being forced to help the Dark Army, he won't hesitate to act! I will bring Lanzor to free you.'

Zorgo looked at the young dragons he had released, 'Go quickly! Find as many other dragons as you can and warn them about the danger they are in. Tell them to gather on Fire Mountain where Lanzor is based. As soon as Lanzor frees the dragons here, we will all meet on Fire Mountain. We must join the good wizards and witches to fight the Dark Army of Deadly Wizards and Witches!'

Zorgo had swiftly found Lanzor. He was holding an urgent meeting with his wizards and witches as he already suspected something sinister was happening. Dragons had been disappearing from the skies.

It was easy to identify Lanzor. He was a head taller than the rest and wore golden robes with a mighty gilded sword at his side. As he raised his head to watch the approaching dragon, his long locks of white gold caught the sun. He looked, every inch, a majestic Warrior Wizard!

Zorgo swooped down and landed in front of Lanzor. The fearsome dragon bent his head and looked directly into Lanzor's eyes and then surveyed the crowd who had gathered around him. Zorgo opened his mind to them all. As they read Zorgo's warning and plea for help, there was a collective shout, 'WE WILL HELP!'

Without a moment's delay, Lanzor threw himself onto Zorgo's back, and turning to the wizards and witches who had gathered around Zorgo, he gave the command, 'PREPARE FOR WAR! WE WILL FORM AN ARMY WITH THE DRAGONS! I WILL GO WITH ZORGO TO FREE THE DRAGONS AND BRING THEM HERE!'

Zorgo soared into the air and with a mighty roar headed back to the caves with Lanzor. They reached the captive dragons before the Deadly Wizards and Witches returned. Using his heavy sword, which he sharpened with a spell, Lanzor sliced through the chains with mighty swipes. As each dragon was released, it headed straight to Fire Mountain where the other dragons were gathering.

Zorgo trained his dragon army to listen for the sounds of spells being chanted and to retaliate with fireballs before the spells were completed. With their superb hearing, they would not be captured again. As highly skilled fliers, they could easily evade a wand being pointed at them. The time had come to face their evil enemy.

And so the mighty Golden Army on dragons was born! In uniforms of gold they lit up the skies … The Great Wizard War began!

No longer having any dragons, the Deadly Wizards and Witches captured warhorses to fight on. The war was long. Although the Golden Army and dragons could have destroyed the Dark Army, this was not in their nature. They repelled the constant attacks and to minimise losses used defensive tactics. They hoped that eventually, the evil side would realise that war was futile and that evil would never win. It was only after the stubborn Dark Warlord fell in battle that the unruly rabble surrendered and agreed to the truce proposed by Lanzor.

Cryptor, having not an ounce of honour in his blood, had no intention of keeping any truce made centuries ago. The war he was about to wage would be won this time … by every foul means possible! His war would be underhand. The new Dark Army would strike secretly and swiftly before an opposing army could be raised!

The Deadly Wizard only needed one dragon for his plan, and its capture was now urgent. With more powerful spells, he would quietly deal with his neighbours until his army arrived to destroy all the villagers. After that, he intended to kill every dragon as well! They had to be punished for having joined the good side in the first war. If it hadn't been for the dragons, the Dark Army would have won. Those dragons had fought with all their fury. Normal evil spells had become useless against them, and the dragons had been formidable in their response. He laughed out loud at the thought of using dragon ingredients in spells that would wipe them out!

Cryptor needed a warhorse again, or maybe two. The journey to find a dragon would be further than the last. And the captive would be bulky.

'I won't call the warhorse that I've just used,' he muttered to himself. 'That bag of bones will still be tired after being half starved to death!'

Waving his wand towards distant mountains in the west he chanted, 'Bellum Equis!'

Once again, Cryptor opened a gap in the evil aura above his house and waited. This time three magnificent warhorses appeared and circled above him. One by one, they landed in front of him, keeping their swords raised.

'I only need two of you,' he said as he scrutinised them carefully. Then he pointed at one. 'Be off with you! You are the smallest. Go! Before I change you into a toad and eat you!' He rocked with evil mirth at the expressions on their faces.

The rejected warhorse needed no further encouragement. It launched itself through the gap in the aura before the evil wizard could change his mind. With a flurry of its swords, it disappeared from sight.

The two remaining warhorses pricked their ears in alarm. There was a loud hissing sound coming from the house. Stamping their hooves on the ground, they nervously backed away. They wanted to be out of this evil place as soon as possible.

To their disgust, Cryptor threw a heavy chain around each of their necks. He chose the larger of the two to mount. Grabbing the red fiery mane and chain, he yelled, 'Go southwest and don't stop till I tell you to!'

They rose through the air. Once clear of the aura, the warhorses soared away into what remained of the dark.

The journey was long and arduous. They crossed the Atlantic Ocean far below them as dawn broke. The morning seemed endless as they were almost keeping pace with the direction of the sun. The further they flew, the hotter it became. Near the equator they picked up the trade winds and increased their speed.

But, after many hours, they were beginning to tire rapidly and to lose height. Cryptor knew they would have to land soon. The winds were taking them towards the Caribbean Sea and Cryptor did not much like the thought of swimming with sharks.

He yelled at the warhorses, 'Turn south! Keep aloft or you'll be shark meat. We'll land in South America!'

Wearily, the two warhorses strained to keep their height above the waves below. Just as they were giving up hope, the shores of Venezuela came into sight.

'There will be people on the beaches!' Cryptor shouted. 'Keep going inland.'

With renewed effort, the warhorses finally found themselves over the remote jungles of Eastern Venezuela. Without being told by Cryptor, they swooped down with their wings flailing and slashing into the vegetation, creating a small clearing to land in. They both sank to the ground, breathing heavily and covered in sweat.

Cryptor dismounted and growled, 'Useless animals!'

The two warhorses looked at each other and then looked up at the sky. If they could muster one last surge of energy, they might escape this cruel wizard.

But Cryptor was quick to prevent this. He grabbed the chains around their necks and tied them to a jabillo tree. 'There'll be no howler monkeys in this tree. Little wonder it's known as the "monkey no-climb tree" with those vicious thorns,' he muttered. 'I'll collect some of its poisonous sap for my potions. And if you two miserable specimens of horsemeat try to escape, I'll make you drink some!'

The warhorses eyed Cryptor nervously. They knew he was capable of killing them! In frustration, they snorted and pawed the ground. They had never been chained up before. Nor had they encountered cruelty like this.

Accepting their fate, the exhausted animals sank to the ground. When they finally fell asleep, it was a disturbed sleep filled with dreams of freedom interrupted by the sounds of the jungle.

There were jaguars and pumas here. Deep coughing barks indicated jaguars were nearby. Fitfully, the warhorses got to their feet with their backs to the tree and prepared to use their mighty wings and hooves to defend themselves.

Cryptor, who never needed much sleep, had propped himself up against a kapok tree. He wasn't worried about jaguars. He had put a protective aura around himself that would last a few more hours. The warhorses could look after themselves, and it would be entertaining to watch them fight a jaguar. But the jaguars, sensing evil, melted away into the night.

'Pity, they've gone,' mused Cryptor. All he could hear now, above the constant hum of insects, were bats higher up in the branches. 'Might just catch a bat or two for breakfast. And maybe smoke a few for the rest of the journey.'

As dawn approached, loud guttural howls could be heard from howler monkeys three miles away. The warhorses were desperate to leave. They could not imagine the creatures making that racket!

Cryptor laughed at them as he finished his breakfast of roasted bats. He spat the bones out into the fire he had made to cook them and leered at the warhorses. 'You'll need more guts than that for where we're going!'

He untied their chains and climbed onto one of them. 'Fly southwest from here. We've a long way to go.'

The warhorses rose high above the tree canopy. They flew over more jungles and towns and finally came to some cloud forests. Looming above this misty and spooky area were the tops of the longest mountain range in the world, the Andes. The snow-capped peaks were breathtakingly beautiful and remote.

Cryptor spotted the ruins of Machu Picchu along the lower peaks and knew they were over Peru. Tourists looking up from the ruins could only make out two small winged shapes high in the sky and assumed they were eagles.

'We're on course,' said Cryptor. 'Keep this direction and we'll soon be over the Pacific Ocean. Somewhere out there are some of the dragons' islands.'

The warhorses' ears pricked up and flattened at the word "dragons". There was only one creature a warhorse never hoped to encounter and that was a dragon. Any kind of dragon.

For many long hours, they flew over endless stretches of water. Hundreds of miles of emptiness lay below them. The warhorses began to fear they might never see land again. They were too heavily built for endless flight, and their wings of swords were heavy.

There was a thick sea fog over the water now. Everything was eerily quiet except for the sound of their wings. Then, on the distant horizon, the tops of trees could be seen emerging from the mist.

'This is it,' Cryptor uttered in a low growl. 'Fly low and land on that island. There may be dragons protecting it from above. They won't spot us in this heavy mist.'

Obediently, the warhorses flew down and

were out of sight just in time! Rising above the treetops were two large dragons with a smaller one in tow. They began to patrol the skies while teaching the smaller dragon to fly.

The warhorses strained to keep their hooves from touching the water as they flew as low as they dared. Their hearts were thumping with fear. A rocky beach appeared through the thick mist, and they landed on the pebbles with a crunch.

'Quiet! You dumb brutes,' Cryptor hissed. 'Make one more sound and we'll all be dead!' He dismounted, grabbed the warhorses' chains and headed inland looking for cover. Coming to some dense undergrowth near a stream, he stopped.

'This will do,' Cryptor whispered hoarsely as he chained each warhorse to a massive rock at the edge of the stream. 'If you make a sound, you will be mincemeat. The dragons will find you! Meanwhile, you have enough to eat and drink here while I am gone. When I return, we will need to make a quick getaway.'

'Those warhorses will fly like devils possessed when they know what we are taking back,' he thought.

The Deadly Wizard combed the island until he found some caves. Crouching behind nearby rocks... he waited, hidden from sight. The three dragons that had been circling the island eventually floated down through the mist.

The two larger ones landed gracefully, and the smaller one landed with a thump. They were a male and a female dragon with their young son. Cryptor's heart almost stopped beating when he realised that this was a family of the most coveted dragons: Chameleon Dragons! He could not believe his luck!

Cryptor quietly spied on them. He needed to see what their routine was and then decide when and how to capture the young dragon.

The Chameleon Dragons went out on regular short patrols. During one, Cryptor crept into the cave they used to see how he could best carry out his plan.

It was dark inside except for a gentle glow that seemed to radiate from some rocks surrounding a large oval shape. He crept closer and saw that it was a large colourful dragon's egg. This would make his life easier! He would steal the egg! Far easier than trying to capture a young dragon …

Before he could act, cracks began to appear in the shell, and there were loud squeals coming from inside. The squeals were amplified in the cave!

His luck had run out! It was hatching … too soon! The dragons were sure to hear the squeals. He had to get out of the cave before they came back. In his rush to get out, the evil wizard didn't notice that behind him, the rocks had started to glow more intensely.

Cryptor only just managed to dive through the entrance and under some bushes when there was a whoosh of air as three dragons swept into the cave.

It was almost impossible to cast spells on adult dragons. When they were within range, they could pick up the first sound of a spell being chanted and could burn you to a frazzle before you completed it. It was a skill they had passed down after the Great Wizard War.

He had to change his plans again. This time, he would capture the newly hatched dragon which would be smaller than its brother.

The next day, Cryptor was amazed to see the adult dragons were already taking the new hatchling out for flying lessons over the sea. It was another young male dragon.

'No wonder Chameleon Dragons are the most feared dragons if they develop so fast!' he thought to himself. *'I must act quickly before this little dragon is too difficult to handle!'*

This was going to be difficult and dangerous. It would be too risky to cast a spell inside the cave. Any sound would be amplified, and there were four dragons with an acute sense of hearing in there. It only needed one of them to hear him and wake up before he finished chanting the spell … then he would be toast! And he would have to make sure the little dragon was unable to make a sound while he captured it.

Cryptor decided to cast a spell to produce

and soundproof a net which he intended to throw over the smallest dragon. When it was dark, he crept to the entrance of the cave. He waited until he was sure the dragons had settled down to sleep. Slowly, he inched inside. Listening carefully, he heard the sound of gentle snoring from the depths of the cave. Holding his breath, the evil wizard slowly approached the sleeping dragons.

The rocks closest to the dragons were glowing with a gentle, deep blue hue. The slumbering shapes of two large and two smaller dragons could just be seen in the glow.

He had to be quick. Holding the corners of the net, Cryptor dropped it over the smallest dragon and wrapped it up tightly. Inside the folds, the little dragon screeched in fright, but no sound could be heard! All was going to plan until, to Cryptor's alarm, the surrounding rocks began to emit a violent red colour. Then, three dragons opened their eyes simultaneously!

In panic, Cryptor charged out of the cave carrying the little dragon. Huge angry roars erupted from the depths of the cave. All hell was breaking loose as the dragons realised their youngest son had been kidnapped! Much as they wanted to roast Cryptor alive, they couldn't risk this in case they hurt the tiny dragon. It was the only reason Cryptor made it out of the cave without being burnt to a cinder!

Once outside, he had only one chance and

that was to quickly cast an invisibility spell over himself and his captive.

'Invisibilia!' he uttered as he pointed his wand at himself and the dragon. Cryptor cursed as he and the little dragon began to disappear into thin air. He had not bargained for those weird rocks raising the alarm! But, unknown to him, it wasn't just the rocks that woke the dragons. It was also the distressed thoughts of the little dragon that alerted them! Evil wizards and witches had never found out that dragons communicated by thought … dragons had never trusted them!

Two massive shapes whooshed out of the cave followed by a smaller one. They soared around breathing huge plumes of fire to light up the darkness as they searched for the little dragon. They knew their youngest was somewhere below, but they just couldn't see him!

Cryptor knew he had to get as far away as possible before the invisibility spell wore off. He didn't realise the soundproof spell was useless.

The warhorses had been sleeping and were woken up by the angry roars and the fiery display in the sky. They realised there were furious dragons on the warpath!

They jumped out of their skins as Cryptor's voice whispered from nowhere, 'Keep very calm if you want to live. I am going to tie a bundle to one of you and mount the other. I will keep you tied loosely together as I cast an invisibility spell over you both. Then, you will fly in tandem!'

The warhorses froze as they felt invisible weights on their backs. Then their chains were linked together. Cryptor pointed his invisible wand at them and quietly chanted, 'Invisibilia!'

He gave them directions as they faded from sight. 'This time we will fly back northwest and over Asia. Ready! Go!'

It was a much longer journey back, and Cryptor had to make many manoeuvres as he tried to shake off the enraged dragons. They had stayed hot on his trail as they could read the little dragon's thoughts, which were cries for help. They just couldn't see Cryptor or their youngster under the invisibility spells. The Deadly Wizard could not understand how the dragons were still able to follow him!

Whenever the dragons got closer, Cryptor made the warhorses peel off in another direction and constantly change their flight altitude. All his cunning skills were needed to escape the furious dragons. He desperately pointed his wand at the dragons, but as soon as he began to chant a spell, they dropped out of range. Their hearing was exceptional!

Inside the net, the little dragon was still struggling and was trying hard to stay awake during the long hours of swooping and swerving through the sky. He was encouraged by the thoughts from his parents as they followed the zigzag route. The dragons were growing ever more frustrated at being unable to use fireballs to incinerate their enemy!

Cryptor grew tired of the little dragon's struggles which were slowing down the other warhorse. He decided to cast a spell to send the dragon to sleep! Pointing his wand in the direction of the other warhorse, he quietly chanted, 'Draco somno!'

The struggling stopped as the little dragon fell into a deep sleep. Although Cryptor didn't realise it, this was a lucky spell for him. The pursuing dragons could no longer pick up their youngster's thoughts. In anguish, all they could do now was to keep heading in the same general direction, towards China, where they might find help in their search.

The warhorses were shattered by the time they reached the Yellow Sea and grateful to see land ahead. China at last! Ahead of them were the Yan Mountains and one of the most amazing sights in the world … The Great Wall of China. Thousands of miles long, it could even be seen from space. This incredible wall snaked over the mountains and far into the distance.

By now, Cryptor's invisibility spells were wearing off. This was not the best place to be, as dragons were much respected by the Chinese for the powers that dragons had. Occasionally, dragons would briefly leave their islands and join in with Chinese ceremonies whenever they were held. Cryptor knew the Chameleon Dragons would alert any dragons here to help them look for their kidnapped youngster. He cursed under his breath. He would have been well clear of China by now if he hadn't needed to keep changing direction!

Cryptor realised they were sitting targets if they stayed in the sky. He urged the warhorses north, passing over the massive Wall. They were now over cultivated land. It wasn't long before Cryptor spotted what he was looking for. He ordered them to land in a muddy field where bales of hemp had been gathered. Cryptor leapt down and dragged the sleeping dragon onto the ground. They were all completely visible now!

Cryptor turned to both warhorses, 'Roll on the ground. Get as much dirt on your manes and tails as possible.'

Miserably, the magnificent red creatures obeyed. Soon, they looked filthy and dishevelled. They were most disheartened by their new appearance. These animals were extremely proud by nature.

Cryptor then loaded as many bales as the warhorses could manage to carry on the swords of their wings and hoisted the little dragon on top of them.

'You look like beasts of burden now,' he uttered, scowling at the warhorses. 'I need to change my robe and hat to complete the disguise.'

Tapping his wizard's hat with his wand, he quietly chanted, 'Conicis paleae!' A conical straw hat appeared on Cryptor's head.

Then Cryptor pointed his wand at his robe chanting, 'Rusticus vestimentum!' He was now standing in rough baggy clothes made of hemp. Cryptor looked like an ordinary Chinese peasant leading two heavily burdened horses.

The party set off on foot, still heading north of the Great Wall.

Cryptor looked back and spotted dragons, circling in the distance. They were helping the Chameleon Dragons in their search. As they flew over, all they noticed down below was a poorly dressed old man leading two scruffy overloaded horses. The little captive dragon was still asleep.

Cryptor and the warhorses trudged heavily on for many hours. He was fuming under his breath and tired of waiting for the dragons to give up their search.

The warhorses were now relieved to be disguised. They knew they would not stand a chance against so many dragons! Despite their weariness, they walked as quickly as they could over the rough ground.

The circling dragons finally decided to give up their search overhead. They concluded that the Deadly Wizard had changed direction. They turned their search to the west instead.

The sky above Cryptor began to empty, much to his relief. Now, Cryptor and the warhorses could resume their flight. The bales of hemp were discarded on the ground. Eagerly, the Warhorses ate huge mouthfuls of the straw while Cryptor was busy changing his clothes back to his wizard's robe and hat. They pricked up their ears when they saw the bundled up dragon move. The spell was wearing off and the little dragon was waking up.

It was risky to cast the same spell in quick succession. The force of the spell would be magnified. This could send the dragon into a sleep of death and Cryptor wanted him alive. Over time, a live dragon would provide far more ingredients!

The Deadly Wizard leapt into action. Keeping the little dragon bundled up, he tied it to a warhorse. Then he climbed onto the other warhorse and shouted, 'Up! Up! Up! Head north! Fly for your lives!' It was far too dangerous to fly west over China if the dragons had headed there.

The warhorses soared into the sky. They had no intention of being chased by dragons again. They flew with every ounce of strength they could muster. To the north lay Mongolia and beyond that Russia. Cryptor knew he would have to stop to let the warhorses feed and rest, or they would never make it back. They would not be able to maintain this speed. The long trek on rough ground had taken its toll.

As they flew high over the vast treeless steppes below, Cryptor directed the warhorses to land on grassland in Mongolia. They collapsed on the ground as they landed. There was little doubt in Cryptor's mind that they could not fly much further. It would take far too long to call up fresh warhorses from the distant mountains they inhabited.

He needed a new plan. They were near the northern Mongolian border. If they could find the railway track connecting to the Trans-Siberian line, they could ride as hitchhikers! Freight trains from China were using this route and would pass through Mongolia, Russia, Belarus, and Poland before finally reaching their destination in Germany.

Cryptor detested the thought of using modern transport, but his options were limited if he wanted to get back quickly. He scoured the horizon. Then turning to the warhorses, he ordered, 'On your feet! We have a train to catch!'

Cryptor forced the unwilling warhorses into the air. From the sky, it was easier to spot the long train approaching across the miles of open grassland. 'There it is! Land on the roof of one of those containers.'

The warhorses swept down and hovered over the train keeping pace with it. They landed on a metallic roof with loud clangs, but there was no one to hear them.

'Lie down and hold tight! I am going to speed this train up!' Cryptor had no intention of waiting two weeks to reach their destination.

He pointed his wand at the engine at the front of the train and shouted, 'OCIUS!'

The train began to pick up speed and started to hurtle along the railway line. The train driver tried to slam on the brakes and slow it down but nothing happened! He began to send out mayday messages in Chinese, warning all traffic in front to clear the line as he was on a runaway train!

The warhorses dug the swords on their wings into the roof of the container to prevent them all being swept off. This weakened the roof and it gave way under them. They found themselves falling amongst boxes of electrical goods. The train was literally flying along the track. Cryptor had no intention of stopping for anything. To speed the train further, Cryptor disengaged the carriages behind them with a sweep of his wand as he chanted, 'Relinquo!'

As the train began travelling at over 250 mph, they struggled to make room for themselves amongst the boxes until Cryptor expelled them through the hole in the roof with a spell. For long uncomfortable hours, the Russian landscape swept passed them, unnoticed in the windowless container.

A Russian armoured train had been alerted and was heading towards Belarus to intercept them, but it had no chance with the speed that the hijacked train was travelling at.

No one could understand how the train hadn't derailed as it flew past in a blur.

At the Belarus-Polish border the railway track gauge would change. The train had to have its bogies changed here in order to complete the journey. Cryptor could hear the train driver screaming dementedly and realised why, just in time. If the train continued at breakneck speed, a terrible crash would be unavoidable on the wrong gauge! Cryptor gave control of the train back to the terrified train driver who was one step away from a nervous breakdown.

The driver slammed on the brakes and with screeching metal and flying sparks, the train ground to a halt just 100 metres short of the border.

Cryptor ordered the warhorses to take to the air again. He had no intention of causing a sensation here. 'Up and out of here! Fly west!' he ordered. 'Don't stop until we're back!'

A crowd had gathered around the train. They couldn't understand the gibbering driver. The military police arrived and were arresting the poor man for hijacking the train when the crowd gasped and pointed to the sky…

Newspapers soon reported the story. They blamed vodka and crowd hysteria for the deluded sightings of flying horses above a hijacked train.

Cryptor wasn't interested in the chaos he was responsible for down below. He urged the warhorses to fly high above Europe. They had recovered their strength during the train ride.

As dusk fell, city lights guided them. They kept well clear of the many airports and well below the flight paths of this highly populated part of the world. At last they found themselves over the North Sea and heading for England. The end of the journey was in sight.

Completely worn out, the Deadly Wizard and the warhorses arrived over Obscura with the captive dragon. All was quiet in the village as they approached Owl Lane and circled above the grey aura over Cryptor's house. As soon as Cryptor opened a hole in the aura, the warhorses dropped through it and stumbled to the ground. They were shaking with weariness and were now as thin as a bone. There were still traces of mud on them, which hadn't been washed off by their sweat.

The Deadly Wizard dismounted. He crossed to the other warhorse and dragged the bundled up dragon off its back.

A loud hissing sound was coming from the house. There was a very hungry snake inside!

Cryptor mimicked the snake and hissed at the warhorses, 'Hssssss! Get out of here, you filthy creatures before I turn you into snake food!'

Alarmed, but finally seeing freedom in sight and with a last mighty effort, both warhorses managed to lift off the ground and disappear into the night. Never again did they want to encounter this monstrously evil wizard. They knew they were lucky to have survived the dragon chase. Lucky to have survived at all!

Cryptor rubbed his hands. He knew this last trip had been worth the trouble. Now he would be unstoppably powerful!

The Deadly Wizard hauled the struggling bundle into his house and released the little dragon in his dungeon. Blinking his huge eyes, the dragon balanced unsteadily on his feet. He was weak with hunger and thirst. In a couple of days he would die without food and water.

Cryptor noticed something around the dragon's neck. It was a medallion inscribed with a name. FANGO. Cryptor snorted as he read it. Two little fangs were protruding from the little dragon's top jaw, which accounted for his name.

'The name Yowler would have suited you better,' growled Cryptor. 'You never stopped yowling and moaning on the way here! I'll give you something to cry about in a minute.'

The evil wizard strode over to a bolted door. He slid back the bolts and disappeared inside a dark side chamber. The little dragon could hear rattling sounds as Cryptor searched through his pile of evil implements. He came out holding a large pair of clippers.

'Come here, you little wretch!' he ordered.

Fango cowered under the Deadly Wizard's glare and crouched down. Mercilessly, Cryptor scooped the little dragon up and chained him to the wall. Cruelly grabbing the little dragon's limbs, he proceeded to cut pieces of his claws off. Fango moaned throughout the whole ordeal.

When Cryptor had finished, he unshackled Fango who now had huge tears rolling down his face. They formed rivulets through the dust that had gathered on him during the long journey.

'You pathetic little baby!' mocked Cryptor. 'You're covered in dirt. Time for a nice, cold shower!'

The evil wizard dragged Fango outside and pointed his wand to a raincloud as he chanted, 'Aquam de caelo!' The heavens opened, and buckets of water rained down!

Within seconds Fango was drenched. The dust on him was completely washed away. The little dragon opened his mouth to swallow as much water as he could. He was dying of thirst.

Cryptor, who had being sheltering in the doorway, reached out and grabbed Fango. Slamming the door behind him, he hauled the little dragon back into the dungeon.

'Go and lie in that corner and don't come out!' Cryptor snarled.

The little dragon edged slowly into the corner. He dreaded what might happen next. He waited in fear. There was a movement on the far side of the dungeon. Fango's eyes opened wide in horror as he made out the shape of a huge snake uncoiling itself. It was lying on the hearth of a large fireplace.

Cryptor also saw the snake move. 'And you,'

he growled at the snake, 'stay there! There is no food for you anymore! But soon it will time for you to go and find it in the village. There are lots of yummy children and pets there … and you will be starving!'

The snake seemed to understand what the evil wizard said and coiled itself up again. But it was already starving. Cryptor laughed. Then something caught his eye on the other side of the hearth. Long pieces of scaly transparent skin were just visible in the shadows. The snake had moulted while Cryptor was away! He pounced on them … more ingredients for his spells!

Fango was eyeing Cryptor warily from his corner of the dungeon. The little dragon did not yet know that he was from a group of the most feared dragons on earth. He was so young and small and looked anything but fearsome. He was vulnerable and terrified! Fango moaned all night feeling isolated and cold in the dungeon.

The snake hissed in agreement, but this only terrified the little dragon more.

THE BLACK SMOKE SPELL

Next door, Felix and Fabia, who had been asleep, were woken up by the sound of heavy rain and new sounds of distress coming from Cryptor's house.

'Cryptor's back,' said Fabia in a low voice. 'What on earth is he up to? I think he started that spell of rain. Whatever can be making those moaning and hissing sounds?'

'We will go over there and confront Cryptor, tomorrow. Something bad is happening inside that house,' said Felix. *'Or something much worse than we can imagine,'* he thought to himself, so he wouldn't alarm Fabia further.

'I think we should put a protective aura around our house, right now, Fabia,' he said as reassuringly as he could.

Fabia nodded in agreement. She fell silent. Felix knew this meant she was very worried. They both got out of bed and picking up their wands, waved these in a circles as they chanted, 'Protege nos!'

A gentle pale aura began to glow and form a protective dome over the house. Felix and Fabia watched it as it glimmered faintly in the moonlight.

Climbing back into bed, they tossed and turned, as the noises from next door continued for the rest of the night. They just couldn't get back to sleep.

Next door, Cryptor had slept extremely well. He woke up in a good mood. He was feeling peckish. The smoked bats he had been snacking on during his journey had run out. There had only been a tin of snails in his larder when he got back. He thought that he thoroughly deserved to make himself a good breakfast. After that, he would deal with those pesky neighbours.

He roared with laughter when he looked outside and saw that a protective aura had been put over their house. 'Those fools have no idea that my magic is now stronger!' he sneered as he strode out of his house.

Cryptor went into a shed and came out holding a fishing net. He approached the pond at the back of his house. It was teeming with the frogs and toads that were now trapped in the garden. They dived to the bottom when they saw Cryptor.

'Come to me, you little beauties,' he cackled. Then with a sweep of his net, Cryptor scooped up half a dozen frogs. He chose three of the fattest ones and dropped the others back into the water.

Returning to the house, he went straight to the dungeon. As soon as Cryptor entered, the snake and the little dragon held their breath. They had learnt that anything Cryptor did would be bad. They both looked miserable as they watched Cryptor preparing his favourite breakfast of fried frogs on toast.

Fango was trying to decide if he was more miserable because of the fate of the frogs or because he was so hungry himself. The two prisoners were starving. Neither of them had had a thing to eat since being captured.

Cryptor looked at them mockingly as he slowly chewed his food. He rose from his table after he had finished.

'Now for the action! I finally have everything necessary to stop those interfering neighbours,' Cryptor muttered.

The Deadly Wizard selected a large cauldron. Setting it on the hearth, he fired it up.

The snake watched him warily but stayed very still. It knew better than to anger the wizard.

Fango looked on from his cold corner of the dungeon. He was standing there, still shivering and wet from Cryptor's cruelty during the night. Fango was so cold, but nothing could induce him to approach the fire that Cryptor had started in the hearth.

Cryptor was almost dancing in evil delight and anticipation. He reached for the first ingredient. It was a large piece of the snake's moulted skin. Cryptor threw it into the cauldron and stirred. Green smoke swirled inside the huge vessel. Then, he threw in the dragon's claw clippings and stirred again. The swirling smoke turned to blazing red. For the final part of his evil spell, Cryptor took out a dagger and sliced off a lock of his own foul hair and tossed it into the cauldron.

He stirred and stirred as he chanted, 'Malum fumi!'

A dark whirlpool of smoke formed. It began to swirl faster and faster. Slowly, tendrils of filthy smoke drifted out of the cauldron. The evil wizard waved his wand and sent the vile black smoke up the dungeon chimney. It penetrated his evil aura, which had been put up with a less powerful spell, and drifted towards the protective aura that Felix and Fabia had placed around their house. The smoke curled through their aura with no trouble at all. Cryptor watched its passage through both auras. With an evil snort of contempt he used his wand to direct the evil smoke down the chimney next door!

'Bonum magicae moritur!' he ranted. It was the final spell for the smoke to end all good magic in the house.

Only two hours earlier, in the house next door, Felix and Fabia had got up early after their sleepless night. Despite the protective aura over them, they were both extremely worried. The disturbing sounds at night had continued until morning. They wanted to confront Cryptor after breakfast when the boys had left for the day.

At the same time that Cryptor had sat down to eat his breakfast, the family finished theirs. Danny and Josh were leaving early to join their great friends, Ginny and Katy, for a full day of birthday celebrations. The girls had promised many magical treats and surprises. The Feisty Four would be together again and the fun could begin!

They had earned the nickname, "The Feisty Four" because they were always seen together practising spells on each other. Danny was smiling at the memory of the spell he had cast to turn Ginny's hair green. It had gone awry and her hair had turned into slithery worms! To get her own back, Ginny had turned Danny's hair into centipedes! It had needed their Spells and Potions teacher, Quirkor, to undo both spells. Quirkor had warned them that one more incorrect letter in one of their spells would have turned them both into spiders! And for their information, female spiders ate male spiders! Both Ginny and Danny had quailed at the thought. Then they decided Quirkor wasn't serious. But he was!

Felix interrupted Danny's musings, 'You'd better hurry, boys. The party's due to start soon. The girls have planned a full programme for the day. You don't want to miss anything.'

Fabia turned to the boys, 'Enjoy yourselves!'

'Thanks, Mom!' they both replied.

As they were leaving, they noticed the protective aura that their parents had put up during the night.

'Is there anything wrong?' asked Danny.

Josh looked puzzled. 'Why do we need one of those?'

'Just testing our magic ability,' Felix replied. He didn't want to alarm the boys until he knew exactly what was happening next door.

'Wow! It looks like a sparkling dome in the sunshine,' said Josh.

'The opposite of that dark aura over Cryptor's house,' Danny observed.

Felix and Fabia waved goodbye as the boys passed through a gap that Felix opened for them in the aura.

When the boys were out of earshot, Felix turned to Fabia. 'I'm relieved the boys are out for the day. When we face Cryptor, anything could happen. Are you ready to go see him now?' he asked. 'I'll just get my wand. I saw yours in the kitchen. We may need them.'

Neither of them suspected that Cryptor was now more powerful. They thought he was just one evil wizard that two of them could handle.

Fabia went into the kitchen. But, by this time, Cryptor had cast his powerful spell, and the evil black smoke had already penetrated both auras. It was now over their house and drifting down the kitchen chimney. With a sudden whoosh, it surged into the kitchen taking Fabia by complete surprise. The foul smoke curled around her. Fabia gasped in shock and the terrible smoke rushed into her mouth and lungs. She stumbled and fell to the ground!

Felix rushed into the kitchen when he heard the commotion. The black smoke immediately forced its way into his nose and lungs. Felix waved his wand at the smoke and tried to utter a spell, but not a sound came out of his mouth. Nothing! To his dismay, he realised he had been stripped of his magical powers! Felix found his way through the choking smoke and helped Fabia to her feet. He held her tightly to stop her trembling.

Fabia reached for her wand and she, too, was unable to utter a spell. Her magical powers had disappeared. They looked at each other in dismay.

'We must be thankful the boys went out and haven't been affected as well,' Felix said grimly. He was relieved that he was able to speak in a normal voice as long as no spell was involved.

'Quickly! We must open all the windows and doors and get rid of this terrible stuff. There mustn't be a single trace of it left when the boys return,' sobbed Fabia. 'They must not breathe it in! Oh! What can we do? Our magical abilities have gone!'

'This must be Cryptor's doing,' Felix said in a low voice. 'He must have used the most powerful spell of all to break through our protective aura. That means he has the strongest ingredients, which can only have come from a dragon and what could be a snake! That explains the noises we've been hearing at night! He has captives! We need to be careful.'

'Cryptor will think he has robbed the boys of their magical abilities, as well as us,' Fabia added. 'He will have assumed they were inside this morning. Thankfully, they won't be back until after the firework display that Ginny and Katy have planned for the evening.'

'We must act quickly. I suggest we go to the village and look for every book there is on dark spells. The Olde Bookshop should have a complete stock. We need to find the spell that took our powers away. Then we should be able to undo it. Cryptor is just one evil wizard, after all. It will be quicker for us to stop him and then warn everybody of his presence here.'

Little did they know that Cryptor's plans already involved a large evil army!

AN AMAZING DAY

Meanwhile, the birthday celebrations had begun. By 9.00 a.m. all the young witches and wizards had arrived. Few knew what to expect, as every house in the village was designed to suit the witches and wizards living in them. They could create worlds within worlds. Space could be expanded and contracted, in their world of magic. Rooms were changed to something new whenever they felt like it or when the spells wore off. It would be exciting to see what Ginny and Katy's house was like, today.

The girls' mother, Gina, greeted them. 'Welcome, everyone! This morning Ginny and Katy will be taking you to experience our new aquarium. You will have lots of surprises and we hope you enjoy them. Choose some swimming costumes and snorkelling equipment to fit you. Have fun! There will be a picnic lunch waiting for you in the garden when you return.

Ginny and Katy's dad, Tristan, had always been fascinated by marine life. For years he had taken secretive trips into the ordinary world, collecting the youngest and smallest marine animals he could manage to transport back at night without being noticed. He nurtured these, in ever-larger aquaria, as they grew. Finally, he had to order a vast aquarium of reinforced glass from Wizzo. It had been built to last and was divided into three sections using internal glass walls. Each section was designed for different species of sea life. It was designed to experience sea life in the water itself! And it wasn't 3D … this was the real thing!

As Ginny and Katy led the party around to the back of their house, they all gasped at the sight before them! This was going to be an incredible experience. Chatting excitedly, the group changed into costumes and selected snorkelling equipment.

When they were ready, Ginny and Katy led them into a chamber that was connected by a glass tunnel to the first section of the huge aquarium. Inside the chamber, a submarine was waiting. It was almost completely transparent. Even the seats were made of reinforced glass.

'We need to stay in this sub while we go through the shark section. Don't be alarmed if a great white tries to take a bite. This sub was made by Wizzo and it's indestructible,' Ginny explained.

Katy led Danny and Josh to the front seats, and Ginny joined them when everyone was seated. Ginny pressed a control button and the door closed with a sigh. Slowly the chamber containing the sub filled with water. The vessel lifted off the ground and a door at the front of the chamber opened. The sub nosed into the tunnel and headed towards the shark tank. At the touch of another button, the glass door at the end of the tunnel slid open. They glided slowly into dimly lit water, and the glass door automatically closed behind them.

They felt they were in the sea. As their eyes grew accustomed to the deep blue water surrounding them, they were mesmerised as large shadowy shapes appeared within inches of them and then, with a flick of a tail, disappeared.

'Did you see that?' exclaimed a boy sitting at the back. 'I think it was a tiger shark! Yes, here it comes again. It has stripes. It IS a tiger shark!'

Everyone turned to look at the huge shape that seemed to blend in with the background.

'They are found in warm shallow waters,' Ginny informed the group. 'They are usually solitary, so this one has his own smaller chamber. You can see the entrance to it over there.' She pointed to a circular tunnel. 'He comes through to join the other sharks when it's feeding time.'

'Do you mean that it's feeding time, now?' asked a girl sitting behind Danny.

'It certainly will be in a few minutes,' said Ginny. 'You are in for quite a show!'

Everyone was glued to the scene outside.

'Look at that! A hammerhead shark! It must be … its head is flattened and look where the eyes are! Weird!' Danny exclaimed.

'It also likes warm waters,' Ginny told them. 'It's found in schools during the day but hunts alone at night.'

'Glad it doesn't go to our school!' joked Josh.

Everyone laughed in relief. They had been unnerved by real monsters swimming so close to them.

'And here comes the biggest of them all!' said Katy, 'Hold tight!'

A huge shape brushed past the submarine. It was a great white shark! The most feared fish in the oceans! Everyone's hair stood on end as its tail lashed out and knocked the submarine sideways. There was a dazed silence as the great creature circled and approached the front of the sub. Its mouth opened wide, displaying rows of serrated teeth. It grasped the pointed end of the sub in its huge mouth and thrashed about. Several screams broke out!

'It's OK!' Ginny shouted. 'This is what he always does! He likes to play fight before feeding time!'

Just then, there were splashes overhead. Shark food was being dropped into the tank. The great white peeled off and joined the other sharks in a feeding frenzy. The water churned as they circled and snapped up the food until there wasn't a scrap left.

Ginny broke the awed silence. 'Any questions?'

'Yes!' said Josh. 'What's the next treat in store for us? Before this excitement kills us all!' he joked.

Everyone laughed … deeply relieved that the sharks had now lost interest in them.

'Wait and see,' replied Ginny as she sat down at the control panel and pressed another button. A door slid open in the wall of the tank and the sub glided through it. It slid shut behind them, stopping any sharks from following them.

They had entered another huge but shallower tank. It resembled a massive swimming pool with a sandy shore on one side. Waves were gently lapping onto the narrow beach.

The sub surfaced and came to rest in the shallows. With a sigh the sub door opened.

'Step out, everyone,' said Ginny. 'The water's lovely. No sharks here. But there are more surprises.'

So far there was no sign of life, and they all relaxed as they waded to the shore.

'We have a special show for you now,' said Katy as she produced a whistle and blew it.

Suddenly, from the far side of the pool, graceful shapes leapt out of the water in formation. It was a pod of four dolphins. They slapped their tails on the water in welcome and greeted the group with clicks, and delighted squeals, and whistling sounds as they blew air through their blowholes. These were the most playful and intelligent sea mammals: bottlenose dolphins!

They danced across the water on their tails, somersaulted and crashed down on the water sending spray all over the spectators. The dolphins were having the time of their lives. But the best was yet to come. They loved to swim with their visitors and take them for rides through the water.

All four of them came into the shallows and looked appealingly at the group while they clicked and whistled.

'What are you waiting for?' cried Katy as she ran into the water and held onto a dolphin's dorsal fin. She whooped with delight as it surged through the water pulling her along.

The group couldn't get enough of the dolphins as they took it in turns to ride them and gambol about in the water with them.

Some of the more confident swimmers put on their masks and snorkels, and the dolphins knew they wanted to dive underwater with them. The dolphins were vigilant for anyone getting into difficulties. If that happened, they would swim under them and lift them up to the surface on their backs.

The morning flew by and it was almost time

for lunch. They said goodbye to the dolphins. The bottlenoses slapped their tails on the water in response as the party climbed back into the sub. The doors closed as they took their seats.

Reversing back into deeper water, Ginny took the controls, and they headed towards the third section of the aquarium. The dolphins swam alongside, and everyone could hear them clicking their goodbyes.

Again, at the touch of a button, a wall slid back, and the sub entered the third and last section of the aquarium. They found themselves in a kaleidoscope of colour. It was a coral reef that was teeming with life. Brilliantly coloured, tiny shoals of fish were darting amidst the coral. There was an endless variety of living creatures.

One of the girls spotted a couple of parrotfish. She giggled as she pointed at their beaklike mouths. They swam up to the window and eyed her sternly. Then in a flash, they were gone, and a shoal of black and white striped damselfish replaced them.

Katy pointed to a much larger triggerfish with orange markings that was busy crushing some shells in its mouth, 'That one can be quite aggressive,' she said.

Christmas tree worms popped their tentacles out to feed. Crabs scuttled around sea urchins and shrimps hovered amongst the algae. Sea turtles circled around as they investigated the sub. Tiny seahorses hovered over the coral.

Ginny was keen to share her knowledge, 'There are more forms of life living on coral reefs than anywhere else on earth and new forms are still being discovered!'

'Can we snorkel in here?' asked Sally. She was a keen swimmer and captain of one the house teams at school.

'Sorry,' Ginny replied. 'The coral is very sensitive and some of those fish have venom in their spiny fins to protect themselves.'

Just as she said that, a striped sea snake emerged from a crevice and using its flattened paddle-shaped tail swam towards them.

'And that attractive snake is the most venomous animal here,' she added.

The sub had now reached the exit door. It slid open to allow the sub to enter another tunnel. This led back to the chamber from where they had started their journey. As soon as the door closed behind them, the water in the chamber drained away. The sub door opened with a sigh.

'Now for our picnic lunch, everybody!' said Katy brightly. 'Follow us!'

There was a fabulous feast laid out on a long trestle table in the garden. Everyone was thirsty and ravenously hungry after all the excitement.

'Help yourselves to lemonade from the fountain,' said Ginny. 'It's icy cold and freshly made this morning. She picked up two glasses, went to a large fountain and held them under the cascade. When they were full of sparkling bubbles, she offered them to Danny and Josh. Everyone was quick to follow. It was delicious.

Taking their drinks, they went to sit on benches on either side of the table and tucked into the feast. The chatter was animated as they discussed what they had enjoyed most in the aquarium. Swimming with dolphins was definitely the best!

The girls' mother came out to join them when they had finished. It was hard to imagine what further excitement could lie in store.

'Tristan will now tell you the plans for this afternoon,' Gina informed them. As she said that, her husband came out with a very tall wizard, who was dressed in a golden robe. There was a huge ripple of excitement. Everyone recognised the white hair and strong features of this stately figure. He was a descendant of the Great Warrior Wizard. Most of his time was spent in the Great Hall on the outskirts of the village. It was said to house a historical collection from the Great Wizard War, and he was the Guardian.

'You will all recognise Lance who lives in the Great Hall,' Tristan said. 'Every year, he takes small groups of young wizards and witches on a tour of the Great Hall and its contents. When he shows you around, you will understand why we need a Guardian!'

'Hello, everyone,' Lance said, smiling warmly. 'You are now old enough to see what

I protect. As this is a special occasion, I have chariots drawn by unicorns waiting to take you to the Great Hall. Come this way.'

There was a surge of excited chatter as the party rose from the table and followed the tall wizard to the waiting convey. White unicorns with golden manes and tails were eagerly awaiting their passengers. Their long horns pointed proudly ahead.

'To any outsider, these unicorns will appear to be ordinary horses while the spell on them lasts,' Lance informed them. He had made sure Obscura's magical creatures were hidden from any passing stranger.

'Five passengers to each chariot,' he ordered. 'Stand at the front and hold on!'

Ginny and Katy led Danny and Josh onto the first chariot. They were delighted to be joined by Lance who gave each of them a rein. 'You don't really need these as the unicorns know the way, but they'll help you to hold on.'

A magical chariot ride was more than enough as a treat but being invited to the Great Hall was beyond anything they had expected!

After checking behind him to see everyone was ready, Lance gave the command, 'Home, my beauties!'

The unicorns whinnied loudly at this acknowledgement. They pricked up their ears and went from a walk to an extended trot and then into a steady canter.

Gina and Tristan watched them until they were out of sight.

'I hope they won't be too overwhelmed by what is in store for them,' murmured Gina.

'We all need to know the secrets that Lance is guarding,' Tristan said as he reassuringly squeezed Gina's hand.

The chariots wound their way around the village perimeter and came to large gates embedded in a high stone wall. As they approached, the gates swung open, and a long drive lay before them. The Great Hall loomed into sight.

It looked more like a medieval fortress with huge towering fortifications than a hall! Due to the surrounding high walls, it could not be seen from the road, and this was the first time the party had set eyes on it. They were silent as they approached the entrance to the fortress.

A drawbridge began to lower over the surrounding moat. A metal portcullis was rising on the inner side of the entrance allowing them to enter. As they passed through, they could see a murder hole above them, which was an opening that was once used to drop rocks or anything else onto invaders trying to storm the fortress!

Danny was curious. 'This is an old fortress. Why is it called the Great Hall?'

Lance turned to him and smiled, 'It does have a great hall inside. So there is a degree of accuracy.

But it was decided, a long time ago, to give the fortress a nondescript name. If anyone overheard a discussion about a fortress, they would have a very different impression of what it might contain. They would assume its contents needed protection. A name such as Great Hall gives the impression that you wish to show off the contents and that there are no secrets inside!'

'And you are the Guardian of the Secrets!' Josh said in an awed voice.

'I am indeed,' replied Lance. 'But these are secrets that are kept within Obscura and only shared with those who reach an age when they can be trusted to keep them.'

The unicorns had come to a halt. Lance addressed the party. 'Come down from the chariots and follow me.'

There was a hushed silence as the group followed Lance through the inner doors and into the great hall. It was dimly lit and felt chilly. As their eyes grew accustomed to the subdued lighting, they could see rows of what appeared to be crystal tombs. In each crystal, a wizard or witch was lying in a perfectly motionless state. They appeared to be in a deep sleep.

With a dramatic sweep of his hands, the Guardian declared, 'Meet your ancestors!'

There was a loud gasp as everyone realised what was meant.

'Don't be afraid! They are all in a state of suspended animation. In your history lessons, you will have heard how many wizards and witches died in the Great Wizard War. What you have not been told is that a wizard or witch's body is not destroyed nor does it decompose. It goes into a state of preservation or suspended animation. They are all waiting for a time when our magic is strong enough to bring them back to life. As time goes by, we are developing stronger spells and each generation has new ideas. Soon, we will reach a point when we can bring our ancestors back. Although spells wear off, there will come a time when they last longer.'

'But why keep this a secret?' asked Ginny.

'There is a downside to this,' explained the Guardian. 'It is not only our good ancestors who are in this state of suspension but all the evil wizards and witches as well!'

'Are they in here, as well?' Katy gasped.

'Not in the great hall, but locked securely in the dungeon below the keep,' Lance replied. 'This is why we must all keep this secret. The evil wizards and witches still out there do not know the location of their ancestors. If they were to find the spell to bring their ancestors back to life before we do, then we will be completely outnumbered. You are learning new magical skills as time goes by. One of you might be the first to discover the spell to bring our own ancestors back!'

There were astonished gasps.

'We haven't come across any evil wizards or witches yet,' stated Katy.

Danny and Josh looked at each other. They both had the same thought, *'Could our new neighbour, Cryptor, be one?'*

'They went into hiding during the Middle Ages, but they are still out there, somewhere,' said Lance.

Before Danny or Josh could voice their suspicions about Cryptor, there was a squeal from the front of the great hall. It was Sally!

She was standing next to a large crystal and said excitedly, 'This is Lanzor, the Great Warrior Wizard! I recognise him from the book about the Great Wizard War! He looks just like you, Lance. Just older!'

Everyone rushed over to gape at the figure.

'There is still more to tell you,' Lance told them quietly. 'I have found a spell just strong enough to bring the essence of a wizard or witch into a cloud of particles that we can communicate with for a short time. As it is your birthday, Ginny,' he continued, 'choose whichever ancestor you would like to talk to!'

Ginny was completely taken aback. Everyone looked at her in expectation.

'It has to be the Great Warrior Wizard,' she said in a hushed voice.

'So be it!' uttered the Guardian as he strode behind the crystals to where a cauldron had been fired up. He threw in several seeds and as they began to smoke he chanted, 'Vivum!' He pointed his wand at the crystal where Lanzor was lying, and wisps of silver smoke drifted over and seeped into it.

Slowly, a faint cloud resembling the prone figure of the Great Warrior Wizard rose from the crystal …

Everyone froze …

'Ask your question,' Lance said to Ginny.

'Oh … please … can you give us advice about the future, Great Warrior … ' Ginny could barely get the words out of her mouth.

Electrically charged particles began to make a static sound and words began to form … 'Be warned, the evil ones are rising up again. You must be prepared for their coming. They are near …'

The static faded away and the faint cloud of particles seeped back into the crystal.

Everyone's hair was standing on end!

'Was that what an ordinary person would call a ghost?' whispered a voice from the back.

'That was a spooky warning!' said Sally. 'Is this all for real? Or is it a party trick?'

Lance looked at them gravely. 'I've asked Lanzor a similar question and his answer was the same. So far nothing has happened. But we must all bear the warning in mind.'

'If you guard the Great Warrior Wizard, do you … do you also guard … the Dark Warlord?' Danny asked in a hushed voice.

'Yes, I do. He has additional security guarding him. You need to know what that is. Follow me … to the keep!

In awed silence, the party trailed behind the tall figure. They had no idea what to expect. Lance stopped when they came to a large reinforced door in the keep. He turned to them. 'This is the biggest secret of all. In size, that is! Don't be afraid, Fordo is very friendly and he is expecting you all. He loves to show off his abilities. But his most important job is defending the keep from anyone or anything attempting to reach the Dark Warlord and his fallen ancestors.'

Lance pointed his wand at the door and chanted, 'Aperta!'

The door slowly swung open. A huge red scaly head appeared in the doorway. Large orange eyes surveyed them from a height.

They all gasped and took a step back. This was a REAL dragon!

'Come out, Fordo. Show us what you can do! I know you love to show off!' said Lance encouragingly.

With his massive chest puffed out, a fierce-looking red dragon emerged and bowed his head theatrically as he spread his wings out above his head.

'Fordo communicates with me by thought. This became possible after he learnt our language when he came here. Fordo will be on guard for three years. After that, he will return to his island home, and I will recruit another dragon to help protect the keep.'

They were still speechless at the sight of the huge dragon. He was awesome!

'Fordo, as you will have learnt at school, is a Fire Dragon. His forefather was Zorgo who led the dragons in the Great Wizard War. He will demonstrate his firepower. If you look at the top of the ramparts, you will see a scarecrow dressed as a Deadly Wizard. It is thirty meters away. On with the show, Fordo!'

The Fire Dragon took a long deep breath and opened his mouth. A long flame of searing heat arched over their heads and incinerated the scarecrow in a flash of sparks. Just a pile of black ash settled where the scarecrow had been.

Everyone clapped and Fordo bowed again. Smoke was still coming out of his nostrils.

'It's Fordo's exercise time. Would anyone like a ride?'

There was another stunned silence. Then they all shouted at once, 'YES, PLEASE!'

'Fordo can take four of you at a time. While you are waiting for your turn, you might want to look at the Dark Warlord in the keep and wander around the fortress.' Lance turned to Ginny, 'As it's your birthday, you may go first with three friends of your choice.'

Trembling with excitement, Ginny pushed Katy, Danny and Josh towards the dragon. She walked up to Fordo and reached up with her hand. Fordo lowered his huge head, and she rubbed him between the eyes. Fordo rumbled in appreciation and closed his eyes.

Lance helped them onto the dragon's back. Fordo waited while Lance attached a collar with four pairs of reins round his neck. He passed a pair of reins to each of them. 'Don't worry if you fall off, Fordo will swoop down and scoop you up! There is an invisibility barrier put up whenever Fordo flies, so you won't be seen from outside these grounds. Enjoy the ride!'

The Fire Dragon swept into the air with powerful strokes. He soared high into the sky, taking them four kilometres above the ground, and then dived down in circles. It was the most exhilarating ride the four had ever experienced. They whooped in delight.

When they landed each of them stroked Fordo. He lapped it all up like an oversized puppy! Fordo was never happier than when he was flying. But he took his job of guarding the diabolical sleeping Dark Warlord very seriously. He would do his best to make sure no enemy would get past him and live if they tried to reach that evil monster!

After their ride, the Feisty Four went to look at the Dark Warlord in the keep. In the gloom his black eyes appeared to be glaring directly at them.

Danny and Josh looked at each other. The evil wizard lying before them resembled Cryptor! Cold shivers ran down their spines …

'We can't ruin the party by telling anyone what we suspect,' Danny whispered to Josh.

'We need proof!' Little did the boys know that Felix and Fabia already had more than enough.

After Fordo had given everyone a ride, the party gathered in the courtyard where Lance was preparing the chariots to take them back. They were buzzing with adrenalin after the afternoon's events.

Fordo was given a huge round of applause, and he took bow after bow as he backed into the keep. The dragon looked at them all and thought, *'I hope you all enjoyed your ride!'*

Everyone gasped and looked at the Fordo, 'Yes! We did!'

The door closed. They were overwhelmed! Fordo had let them read his thoughts! They would never forget this day!

Lance turned to face the party. 'Remember what I am about to tell you! You are about to become Keepers of the Secrets held in the Great Hall! Never openly discuss what you have seen when you leave. You may be overheard. But if you are sure that only Keepers of the Secret are present and you need to discuss what lies within these walls, it is advisable to soundproof the area you are in. All your parents and elders are already Keepers of the Secrets. Any younger brothers and sisters, who have not yet been to the Great Hall, are still too young to understand that this is important for our security. So, place your right hand over your heart and promise me now that you will keep the secrets of the Great Hall!'

They all placed their right hands over their hearts and solemnly said, 'We promise to keep the secrets of the Great Hall.'

The Guardian looked at each of them as they made their promise and inclined his head. 'Now it is time for the return journey. Follow me.'

Lance led them to the chariots where the unicorns were waiting. 'Climb on board, everyone!'

On the return journey, the only discussions were about the exhilarating ride. No mention was made that a secret dragon was involved.

When the chariots arrived at the end of the girls' drive, everyone thanked Lance.

'Keep working on those new spells!' were the last words Lance said as the unicorns headed home. *'We may need them soon,'* he thought.

The sun was setting and there was the last celebration of the day to enjoy. Tristan had organised a firework display. An invisibility shield had been erected on the outer perimeter. The fireworks would only be visible from the garden.

The picnic table had been cleared, and a magnificent birthday cake that Fabia had made was on it. Candles hovered around it, lighting it up.

Tristan lit a fuse that triggered the fireworks. As silver and gold stars lit up the sky, everyone sang 'Happy Birthday' to Ginny. She blew out the candles and made a wish.

The fireworks died down and they all clapped. Pieces of cake were handed out. It had been the most amazing party and a day of nonstop excitement. They were now ready for a peaceful night's sleep. But, for two of them, that was not to be …

When the boys returned home, they found their parents waiting for them. From the expression on their parents' faces, they knew something terrible had happened.

'We have bad news, boys,' Felix told them, gravely. 'A spell cast by Cryptor has robbed us of our magical powers. Our protective aura was penetrated by evil black smoke. We were taken by surprise and breathed it in. The most powerful ingredients must have been used.'

'We have both heard some unusual noises recently. Sounds of hissing that began a few days ago and moaning that started last night suggest he has captives in his house. He must be using these captives to supply the ingredients for such a spell,' Fabia said. 'We believe the smoke was meant for the four of us. You boys still have your powers, and Cryptor does not know you were not exposed to the smoke he sent here. We need to rely on you both until we can break the spell.'

Danny clenched his fists. 'Josh and I will do everything we can to help!'

'Yes,' Josh added, 'we'll do whatever it takes. I thought I heard strange noises last night, coming from next door.'

'Why didn't you mention that, Josh?' asked Fabia.

'I was half asleep and thought it might have been a nightmare. I didn't want to worry you if it was nothing,' Josh replied.

'That makes four of us!' exclaimed Danny. 'I also heard them. We have more evidence that Cryptor is evil. Today Josh and I went to the Great Hall.'

'We know the promise you made there. We made the same promise years ago. We can speak freely amongst ourselves,' said Felix.

Josh spoke very quietly, 'We saw the Dark Warlord being guarded by a Fire Dragon. Cryptor looks just like him. He must be an evil descendant!'

'But what was worse,' Danny added, 'was that the Great Warrior Wizard was able to warn us that the evil ones are rising up again, and we must be prepared for their coming. The last part of the warning was that they are near …'

'Lance said he was given the same message by the Great Warrior Wizard,' Josh whispered.

This was serious. 'Without a doubt, Cryptor is up to something evil and dangerous. So far, he is the only evil wizard here. We must try to stop him as soon as possible. It will take too long to call a village meeting and explain the situation … by then it could be too late! Cryptor must be stopped tonight! Fabia and I need to regain our powers as well. We can't wait for Cryptor's spell on us to wear off. Any further spells he casts will be stronger,' Felix said urgently.

'While you were at the party, we have been searching for the spell Cryptor cast. We brought back every volume on dark spells from The Olde Bookshop. There's only one volume left to finish looking through. The spell must be in it,' Fabia said hopefully.

The boys saw a pile of old books on the table. One was open and was nothing like a modern 3D book. All four gathered around it and Felix slowly turned the pages. They grimaced as they read the deadly contents. Fabia shivered. 'How could so much evil be created?'

A few pages before the end of the book, Felix exclaimed, 'At last! This is it! The Black Smoke Spell! Just look at those ingredients! He used snakeskin and dragon claw clippings! The other ingredient would have been Cryptor's own hair, according to this!'

'So Cryptor must have a captive snake, which accounts for the hissing noises we have heard,' gasped Fabia.

'And those moaning sounds?' asked Josh quizzically. 'They don't sound anything like a dragon!'

'Oh! It could be a very young dragon that hasn't learnt to defend itself yet. The poor little thing must be terrified,' suggested Fabia.

'No wonder he was away for so long. I'm amazed he managed to capture one without being fried alive! All dragons detest evil wizards!' Felix exclaimed.

'So, to break the spell on us, we will need the same ingredients except for the evil hair. If we substitute hair from a good wizard, it should produce white smoke which will restore our powers when we breathe it in!' Fabia said excitedly. 'And those ingredients will make our spells more powerful, too!'

'We still have our wizard powers.' said Danny. 'Josh and I can use our hair for the spell. The difficult part will be obtaining the other ingredients.'

'We have to get into Cryptor's house as soon as possible,' murmured Josh in a low voice.

'Cryptor will definitely go out tonight to create havoc somewhere as he thinks we cannot stop his evil spells now,' Felix said grimly. 'If you manage to get into his house, I dread to think what you might find there, boys. You must both be very careful, and if it is too dangerous you must come back immediately. Find your darkest robes and wear the hoods.'

The boys went up to their bedrooms to change. These were no ordinary bedrooms. Each boy was allowed to arrange his room exactly as he wanted it and to change it as often as he liked or after the spell on it wore off. They could even change the size of the rooms.

Danny was interested in stars and planets, and his room resembled a domed planetarium. Miniature holograms of the solar system were orbiting around a sun, which acted as a light.

In the centre there was a launch pad with a spaceship on it! Danny walked up to the spaceship and climbed through a hatch. It was like entering another room. It was much larger inside than it looked from the outside. He passed a bunk bed where he slept and opened a compartment. Taking out his midnight blue school robe, he changed into it.

Meanwhile, Josh was in his bedroom which he had designed as a racing track! There were all types of hologram cars racing around it. In the pit stop there was a solid car, larger than the others, and it had a bed in it! Josh went to a storage cupboard at the side and changed from his party robe into a school robe, as well. He went to find Danny and they headed back downstairs.

After what had happened to their mom and dad, the two boys were determined to stop Cryptor. They vowed they would find the ingredients for the spell that would bring back their parents' magical abilities again.

The family quietly waited for Cryptor to go out on his trouble-making trip. Eventually, they saw the Deadly Wizard step outside his house and point his wand in a southerly direction. They couldn't hear the spell he chanted, but they saw him open his chained gates. A magnificent griffin landed on the road outside his gates and bounded in. As it stood under the moonlight, they could clearly see this amazing creature, which had the body, tail and back legs of a lion combined with the head, wings and legs of an eagle at the front!

'Cryptor certainly has the most powerful spells in his hands now,' Felix said worriedly. 'He is now able to call up the king of the beasts, and the king of the birds … in one magical creature. He must be stopped at all costs!'

They watched Cryptor walk up to the griffin. He threw a chain around its neck and hauled himself onto its back. With its powerful back legs, the griffin lunged through the gate. Its eagle's wings opened up when they were clear of the bramble walls and they took to the skies. The gates shut and the chains rattled back into place securing the entrance against intruders.

THE RESCUE

The whole family knew they had to work quickly.

'The bramble barrier has dark magical properties. It will be impossible to go through it, and there is an evil aura over Cryptor's house. His gate is securely locked. The only possible way in would be to tunnel under the brambles and into the garden,' said Felix.

'Boys, it's time to cast a spell,' said Fabia. 'Call up a giant badger.'

'Josh, you do it,' Danny urged. 'You've just learnt animal spells in Quirkor's class.'

Josh pointed his wand at the ground and uttered, 'Meles!' He was eager to prove he could remember the spell for a badger.

The ground under their feet started to tremble and a mound of earth appeared. Then a large white head with two black stripes popped up and looked at them quizzically. It was a large, friendly animal, and it was only too delighted to help.

The boys pointed to where they wanted a tunnel, and in a flash the badger set to work in a flurry of dust and soil. In no time at all, a mound of earth appeared on the other side of the brambles, and the badger emerged in Cryptor's garden, looking very pleased with itself.

'Quick, let's get going,' Danny said to Josh.

'Remember to come back if there is any sign of danger,' warned Fabia.

The boys bravely crawled into the dark tunnel lighting the way with their wands. As they reached the halfway point, they could feel the temperature drop and knew they were under the bramble fence. Their parents watched the boys scramble out on the other side. A badger's tunnel was safer than one created by a spell which might have worn off while the boys were inside it!

The badger came up and nuzzled them.

'Thank you for helping us,' said Danny.

'We may need your help again,' Josh added. 'Please wait here for a bit.'

The badger looked nervously at Cryptor's shadowy house and shivered. Reluctantly, it sat down.

There was an eerie sound of loud hissing and moaning coming from the house. The boys looked at each other. They had to find out what was making those pitiful noises. Pulling the hoods of their robes low over their heads, they blended into the darkness. As noiselessly as possible, they moved towards the only window at the front of Cryptor's house. All the others had been bricked up.

Holding their breath, they peered through the glass. As their eyes grew accustomed to the dark, they could make out what appeared to be a large sunken dungeon. There was a huge fireplace at the far end with some glowing embers that threw off just enough light for them to make out two shapes.

Something very long was slowly slithering along the stone floor in a serpentlike motion. It was approaching a shape that was almost as tall as the boys but rounder. They could just see claws on its feet and small wings on its back. It was a young dragon! A low groan was coming from the little dragon as it began to shake in fear at what could only be a massive snake approaching it!

A hissing sound came from the snake as its tongue flicked in and out of its mouth.

The boys looked at each in horror.

'That snake is going to eat the dragon. It's young and terrified,' whispered Josh

'We have to rescue it before it's too late,' Danny whispered urgently. 'I know! I'll cast a spell to slow the snake down!' He pointed his wand through the window and chanted in a low voice, 'Retardo!'

The spell took instant effect. The snake could only move in slow motion now. But the little dragon had closed its eyes in fear and was standing petrified in one spot.

'We've got to get inside, Josh!' Danny said in alarm. 'But the house is sure to be booby trapped by Cryptor!'

'I'll ask the badger to tunnel into the dungeon!' Josh said.

He turned and ran to the badger and indicated where he wanted the animal to dig. 'Please help!' Josh pleaded.

The giant badger liked these boys. So, despite its anxiety, it began to frenziedly dig a tunnel under the house and into the basement. As soon as soil had stopped flying out, both boys crawled after the badger as fast as they could.

Meanwhile, the snake was still inching towards the little dragon, who was sobbing uncontrollably. As the snake slowly opened its huge cavernous mouth, the boys reached the little dragon and pulled it out of reach.

This was too much for the poor badger! Never in its life had it seen a snake that size. It shot back down its tunnel and stood trembling in Cryptor's garden.

'That was a close shave!' whispered Danny.

'You can say that, again!' exclaimed Josh. 'That is some monster of a snake!'

Danny's eyes wandered from the snake to Cryptor's table. In the faint glow he could see vials and jars which had to contain the ingredients for Cryptor's evil spells. He looked carefully at the contents. 'I think I can see snakeskin in one of those jars over there.

We need that for our good spell!' Danny said excitedly and ran to get it.

Josh was gently leading the little dragon to the entrance of the tunnel. It had stopped crying and was looking at them with huge green eyes.

'We've come to rescue you,' Danny said softly. 'Follow us down this tunnel.'

Josh stroked the little dragon. 'I'll go first, then the dragon should see it's alright to follow.' He crawled into the hole using his wand as a torch for the dragon to follow.

By now, the huge snake was turning around and staring at them with mesmerising yellow eyes. The little dragon needed no further encouragement and dived after Josh! Danny was quick to follow.

The giant badger stared at the dusty trio as they emerged next to him. It was still suffering from shock. Badgers sometimes encountered snakes in their tunnels, but this snake was the stuff of nightmares! Then the badger saw the jar Danny was carrying. It shuddered in disgust, wondering what on earth the boys wanted snakeskin for.

Josh went up to soothe and reassure the badger. 'Thank you for helping us.'

These were the first friendly voices the little dragon had heard since being captured. There was hope at last. These boys could be trusted. They had risked their lives in that terrible dungeon.

'We'd better get back to our house before Cryptor returns,' Danny urged.

'You lead the way,' Josh said to the badger.

Only too happy to leave this terrifying place, the badger entered the tunnel leading under the bramble barrier. The other three followed and were greeted with relief by Felix and Fabia.

Now there was time to look at the little dragon more closely. Felix spotted the medallion around the dragon's neck. He reached out and read it. 'Fango. Is that your name?' This was a male dragon and certainly very young! He had smooth green skin and tiny stumps on his head that would grow into horns. His eyes were enormous and would be able to see for miles.

The little dragon seemed to understand. He nodded and a huge tear began to roll out of one eye.

'We'll make sure you are safe now, Fango,' Fabia said gently and wiped Fango's tear away. Another tear replaced it … but this time it was a tear of happiness and relief.

'It's hard to tell what sort of dragon Fango is. When they are so young, most dragons look the same,' Felix said quietly.

Fango looked at them with his huge eyes and flapped his small wings. Everything felt warm and friendly here. So different to the place next door. These were the only humans the little dragon had encountered, other than the evil wizard: thankfully, they were kind.

Suddenly they all heard a loud hissing noise next door. The huge snake had crawled out of the dungeon tunnel and was heading towards the tunnel leading to their house. The spell on it had worn off! In the moonlight it was even larger than it had looked in the dark.

'Where on earth did Cryptor find that snake?' gasped Fabia.

The giant badger leapt in alarm! It did not want to face that creature again! Without being asked, it started to frantically dig soil back into the tunnel to block it. That monster had to be stopped! Frustrated hissing came from the other side of the brambles when the snake found its way barred.

None of them knew that Cryptor had been starving the snake, and that it was hunger that had made the snake want to eat the dragon. They didn't realise that the snake was also trying to escape from Cryptor. It wasn't chasing them. It was desperate and did not want to remain a captive!

'Cryptor will be outraged when he finds his snake in the garden. Luckily, it can't escape into the village due to the bramble walls and chained gate. It will distract Cryptor before he discovers Fango is missing and give us a bit more time,' said Felix.

'Everyone go inside the house before Cryptor returns,' urged Fabia. 'Bring the badger: he deserves a special treat for his help.'

CRYPTOR THE RAT

It was light and warm in the kitchen. Fango looked around with his enormous eyes as the giant badger came up to sniff him. Never having seen a dragon before, it was curious and nuzzled Fango gently. The little dragon knew the badger had helped to save him. He reached out and stroked the badger's head. It made everyone smile.

'I hate to interrupt, but you boys need to cast the spell for us to regain our powers as soon as possible,' Felix said urgently. 'I see you managed to get some of Cryptor's snakeskin. All you need now is the other powerful ingredient which, hopefully, Fango will help with.'

'While you boys set up a cauldron, I'll give Fango and the badger something to eat,' said Fabia. 'I doubt Cryptor would have bothered to feed Fango.'

She put a large mug of warm milk and a bowl of porridge sweetened with honey on the kitchen table and beckoned to Fango. The little dragon didn't need to be asked twice. Eagerly, he hurried to the table and picked up the mug. Opening his mouth he downed the milk in one gulp! Fabia filled it up again. Then Fango polished off the porridge. He closed his eyes in bliss as he savoured the delicious sweetness.

'That evil wizard must have starved you,' Felix said sternly.

Fabia placed a large bowl of nuts and cereal in front of the giant badger. The badger decided there and then that he would live in their garden from now on.

After the boys had set up the cauldron on the hearth and lit a fire under it, Danny turned to Fango and said, 'We need some dragon claw clippings for a powerful spell. I promise we won't hurt you. We have to stop Cryptor casting evil spells and it can only be done with your help. Mom and dad need to regain the magical powers that Cryptor took away. Then the four of us can cast a strong spell against Cryptor to stop him from capturing you again. Please help us.'

Fango frowned and appeared to understand. Cryptor had hurt him and had been rough when he forcibly cut his claws, but he trusted the boys and wanted to help them in return. He was prepared to do anything to avoid becoming Cryptor's prisoner again. So Fango stretched out his forelimbs and Danny gently clipped a few pieces from the dragon's claws. It didn't hurt at all.

Josh opened the jar of snakeskin and stripped a piece off. There would be plenty left over if they needed powerful spells in the future. He then carefully cut off a lock of his hair and passed the scissors to Danny who did the same.

The boys finally had the three vital ingredients for their spell. They checked that the cauldron was fully fired up. Felix and Fabia quietly crossed their fingers. Fango and the badger watched in fascination.

'Now for the spell!' Danny said.

In went the snakeskin. Green smoke began to swirl around the cauldron. In went the dragon claws. The swirling smoke turned a vibrant red. In went their locks of hair. Danny and Josh took turns to stir.

Suddenly from outside, they all heard the most outrageous shrieking and ranting followed by rumbles of thunder and lightning. The snake was hissing its lungs out.

'Oh no! Cryptor is back!' moaned Fabia.

'Hurry boys, or all will be lost!' Felix urged.

The boys stirred frantically. A whirlpool began to eddy around the cauldron going faster and faster. Danny and Josh pointed their wands and chanted, 'Fumus albus!'

The smoke turned to brilliant white as it whirled around and tendrils of it rose up and filled the kitchen. The boys' parents quickly breathed in huge lungfuls. They felt all their magical powers returning and picked up their wands.

'We must now cast the spell for the white smoke to end Cryptor's evil magic!'

Felix and Fabia waved their wands at the white smoke still coming out of the cauldron as they chanted, 'Perdere mala!'

'There is no time to lose,' ordered Felix. 'Everyone point your wands and direct the smoke out and into Cryptor's house. He is inside now and must have taken the snake with him as the hissing has become very faint. This smoke will be powerful enough to pass through both auras which were made with weaker spells!'

All four pointed their wands at the smoke emerging from the cauldron and directed it through their door, through the auras and down the chimney of Cryptor's house. It poured into the dungeon where Cryptor had discovered the dragon was missing. He was ranting with rage as he surveyed the hole in the dungeon floor and the tunnel through which the dragon had escaped.

'I'll kill them all! The whole lot of them!' he roared. 'I went to the ends of the earth for that wimp of a dragon! I WILL KILL THE MISERABLE RATS WHO STOLE MY DRAGON! THOSE NEIGHBOURS WILL ALL DIE!'

In the gloom, he didn't notice the smoke rushing in, and he took a huge breath to utter another threat. As he opened his foul mouth, the white smoke rushed in and down into his lungs. It was only then he realised what was happening. He choked.

Reaching for his wand, he tried to utter a death spell. Nothing happened! Not one evil magic word came out of his malign mouth. He had been robbed of his terrible powers! Cryptor stormed up and down the dungeon and found he could only shout and scream in fury when there was no magic involved!

The snake eyed the evil wizard with interest. It sensed the tables were turning and Cryptor would now be at its mercy. It was now so hungry that it decided to eat this foul-smelling, festering piece of evil! The snake slithered silently towards Cryptor and raised its head to strike …

Just in time, Cryptor realised the danger he was in. He leapt up the dungeon steps yelling in fury. He rushed out of the house, slamming the door behind him and ran up to the bramble barrier separating the two houses.

Cryptor screamed at his neighbours at the top of his lungs, 'I'LL KILL YOU ALL! This spell will wear off and then you will die. Those two brats of yours will die first. I'll make them suffer a fate worse than death. I'll turn them into rats and feed them to my snake while you watch!'

In the house next door, the family heard his tantrums and smiled. They looked at each other thinking exactly the same thing! The four of them walked outside and faced Cryptor. They all pointed their wands at the evil wizard and chanted, 'Rattus!'

Cryptor's hat and robe collapsed into a pile on the ground. A large black rat crawled out from under the pile and eyed them maliciously.

'I would keep well out the way of your snake, Cryptor. You've become a prisoner in your own house and grounds. You created an impenetrable barrier and gate, and anyone trying to rescue you through your evil aura will be incinerated,' Felix told him sternly. 'You need a taste of your own medicine!'

'Talking of taste,' Fabia added as she looked through the brambles at the rat, 'we aren't as cruel as you, Cryptor. We will feed your snake regularly and give you rat pellets to eat. Now that you've closed the door to your house, you are stuck outside. But you'll have water to drink from your pond, and you can shower in the rain. We don't recommend you go down the tunnel to your dungeon as we will keep a nice fire burning to keep the snake warm down there. The snake might just fancy a quick snack if you appear!'

In his rat's body, Cryptor squeaked in outrage as he glanced up at his door handle, which was well out of reach.

Turning to her family, Fabia said, 'It is so insulting for rats to have that evil wizard take on their bodily form. They are such intelligent animals.'

'Being intelligent, I am sure they would understand,' Felix replied.

Fango had been watching anxiously, and the boys were sure his eyes were now twinkling with delight. Justice had been done ... for the present.

WELCOMING FANGO

The night of Fango's rescue had drawn to a close. No one wanted to sleep after so much excitement and it would soon be daylight anyway. But there was one exception … the giant badger had dug itself a den in their garden and had curled up fast asleep, happy in its new home.

Danny, Josh and their parents had a traumatised little dragon to take care of. Fango was too young to fend for himself. He needed time to develop into a dragon they could identify, and then they could search for his parents. They were hoping Cryptor hadn't killed them during the capture.

Fango would need to be fed properly, and his wings would need to grow much larger to be able to cope with long flights. After being cruelly treated by Cryptor, he needed to regain his confidence. And the family needed to win Fango's trust. In his short life, Fango had little experience of the world outside his dragon home.

Fango seemed to understand what they said to him. He was probably learning their language. When Fango mastered it, they hoped he would trust them enough and allow them to read his thoughts. They needed to be patient until then.

But right now they all had to deal with the danger Cryptor had been planning.

Felix faced the family with a serious expression. 'I am going to the Great Hall to inform Lance of these developments. He needs to know an evil wizard has been active here. The Great Warrior Wizard's warning of an evil uprising must involve Cryptor. There is a high possibility of an attack on the village. Cryptor has been up to something evil on his nightly trips, and we have only stopped his plans for as long as our spells last. While I am away this morning, could you boys change the sign on Cryptor's gate in case other evil wizards and witches arrive looking for him? Once everyone decides how to deal with Cryptor, we'll take down his brambles and aura. Until then, they serve to keep him in.'

'When you've finished the sign, why don't you show Fango his new surroundings,' said Fabia, trying to lighten the atmosphere. 'Start with the gardens. After being in that horrible dungeon, it will do Fango a lot of good to see some daylight.'

'Great idea, Mom,' replied Danny. 'We could all do with some sun after Cryptor's storms.'

The boys led Fango outside onto the lawn. Fango sat down and then rolled on the grass like a puppy. It felt soft and welcoming after the cold stone floors of the dungeon. They stroked and tickled Fango and his tail thumped the ground in pleasure. It was good to feel safe again.

'What do you think we should change Cryptor's sign to?' asked Josh.

'Mm… DANGER! CONDEMNED BUILDING! That suggests no one would be living in it!'

Josh nodded enthusiastically. 'You cast a spell to write it, and I'll cast a spell to wipe out the old sign!'

They walked around to Cryptor's chained gate.

'I wonder why Cryptor had a sign with his name on it. Dumb if you ask me!' Josh said.

'Evil wizards and witches are a stupid bunch. They have never acted logically!' Danny replied. 'Guess he wanted other foul friends of his to find him here.'

Josh shuddered at the thought. Fango, who was sticking close to his new friends, looked around worriedly.

Josh pointed his wand at the sign and chanted, 'Delens scripto!' The letters on Cryptor's sign faded away.

Fango watched in fascination and carefully listened to the boys as they cast their spells and the new sign was finished. The little dragon's brain was working overtime as he learned more and more of their language. There was nothing nasty in their speech, unlike the abuse Cryptor had yelled at him.

The boys noticed that Fango was studying them and smiled. They would take good care of him.

'You must still be hungry, Fango. Let's go find some fresh food for you,' said Danny

'Follow us,' Josh told the little dragon. 'You won't believe your eyes!'

They returned to their garden and the boys showed Fango some of the incredible plants in it. Tropical mango, papaya and avocado trees were growing amongst watermelons and strawberries. They wandered around the oversized plants.

'Choose whatever you'd like to eat, Fango. It's all good,' said Josh.

Fango wasn't sure where to start.

Danny went over to a huge watermelon and tapped it with his wand. It split into three pieces. He gave Fango and Josh a piece each and then took a bite out of his. Fango popped his whole portion into his mouth and swallowed it, skin and all! His eyes lit up! It was amazingly thirst-quenching and tasty! The little dragon needed no more persuasion, and he went about tasting whatever he came across. For a little dragon, he had a huge appetite!

The boys watched him in awe. He was already looking more confident. They would bring Fango here every day. There was much, much more he would enjoy eating, and he needed to grow as quickly as possible.

'We must make sure we feed the snake, as well,' whispered Danny. 'When he's hungry, he might eat anything.' He didn't want Fango to hear this comment.

When Fango finally stopped eating, Josh turned to him and asked, 'Are you old enough to breath fire, Fango?'

Now that Fango was full of food and fuelled up, he opened his mouth and with all his might shot out a long flame of fire! He had tried to do that in the dungeon but after being starved, he couldn't even produce smoke.

'Wow, Fango! You must practice that and learn to defend yourself,' said Danny. 'We'll soon have you big and strong enough to escape capture by Cryptor after he returns to his old evil self.'

When the little dragon heard the name Cryptor, his head dropped. The boys looked at each other with the same determined thought in mind.

'We are a team now, Fango. We'll stick together and you'll never be left to face Cryptor on your own.'

The little dragon's face lit up. He completely understood their thoughts!

They spent the rest of the morning exploring the never-ending enchanted garden. Space could be magically stretched in Obscura. They followed a stream at the bottom of the garden. It led to a waterfall that spilled into a crystal blue pool. The boys had a rowing boat moored there.

'Climb in, Fango,' said Danny. 'We'll row and you sit back and enjoy the ride.'

Fango looked doubtfully at the water. Fire breathing dragons and water didn't mix well. His parents had already taught him that.

Josh reassured him. 'It's alright, Fango. We never capsize the boat.'

The little dragon stepped on board and sat down on the floor. He was still nervous. The boys realised that Fango couldn't swim. They would teach Fango. The little dragon read their thoughts and doubted that was possible.

Danny and Josh took an oar each and pulled away from the bank. To Fango's surprise they headed for the waterfall. They carefully rowed behind the cascading water and entered a cavern. The whole area was bathed in a pale green glow.

'These are enchanted rocks,' explained Danny. 'They glow and change colour according to the mood they are in. There are stories that dragons that could do the same once lived here. No one knows why the dragons left. Maybe they went to fight in the Great Wizard War. That was a long terrible war when all dragons joined forces with good wizards and witches to fight the evil Dark Army.'

It was difficult for the boys to know how much Fango could understand, but the little dragon was listening intently.

The boat floated gently towards the rocks. 'Would you like to touch one of the rocks, Fango?' Josh asked.

The little dragon nodded his head, and as they passed close to one, Fango reached out and felt it. The rock responded in the most amazing way. It started to emit brilliant fireworks that exploded all over the cavern.

Danny gasped! 'The rocks have never done that before. Even when we touch them!'

'It must be because you are a dragon and they are welcoming you back!' Josh said in excitement.

The three watched the spectacular firework display in awe. Every colour imaginable was exploding into stars around them. Both boys looked closely at Fango. He was a long way from resembling a fierce adult dragon. It would be amazing to watch Fango change as he grew!

When the brilliant show was over, Danny said, 'That was fantastic. We'll all come back here again. Now we must go home and show you where you will be living with us, Fango.'

By the time they reached the house Felix had returned. He had a grave expression on his face. 'Lance was expecting to hear bad news when I met him. He sensed that the warnings about an evil uprising were coming true. A meeting is being called in the Village Hall, tonight, when Lance will outline his plans to everyone. All children will be told not to go out alone. If they have to go out, then an adult must be with them. He suspects Cryptor's followers will be out looking for him, and sooner or later, they will find this village. Until we have our defences in place, we are to carry on as normal and pretend we are unaware of any danger in case we are being observed.'

The boys were quiet while they absorbed this news. Things were far from normal here. Next door there was a massive snake and an evil rat imprisoned by thorn walls and an evil aura. And here, they had a young fire-breathing dragon. Things couldn't be less normal!

To cheer everyone up, Fabia decided to set up a picnic table in the shade of some trees. It was out of sight from the road. The giant badger emerged sleepily from his den and decided to continue snoozing under the table. He had hopes that he would continue to be rewarded with tasty tit bits. Soon, the table was overflowing with food. The little dragon eyed it with curiosity.

'Fango, we never need to kill animals for food,' Fabia explained. 'The village keeps dairy cows for milk, butter and cheese, and chickens for eggs. Those sausages on the table are made from soya plants that we grow, and they are rich in protein. We have every variety of nut and fruit trees as well as vegetables in the village. We hope you will enjoy our food.'

'Help yourselves, everyone,' said Felix as he joined them outside.

Fango went up and took a few sausages and boiled eggs. He licked his lips. The sausages were delicious. Then he helped himself to a pile of cheese sandwiches. He nibbled one. Fango wasn't so sure about the taste of these, so he opened his mouth and blew out a flame. It toasted his plate of cheese sandwiches. Now they tasted much better! Everyone watched him with amusement.

'Please toast some of those sandwiches for us, too,' Danny requested.

Fango was only too happy to be able to do something for the boys.

No one had noticed that while they were eating, Cryptor's snake had come outside via the tunnel under the dungeon and was in the garden next door. When Cryptor saw it emerge, he scurried away to hide under the roots of a tree. His two little black eyes stared in silent fury as the snake found a sunny spot to bask in. How dare that snake terrorise him out here as well as in the dungeon. It was freezing cold in the garden at night, while that reptile had a warm fire inside. When he returned to his wizard form, he would vent every evil spell he knew on those boys, their parents and the whole village. And that snake and dragon would be severely punished and tortured if he decided to keep them alive.

Cryptor knew that his new Dark Army would start a search for him and eventually find this village, but they would be looking for an evil wizard, not a rat! His anger knew no bounds as he hid amongst the roots mentally recalling every cruel spell he would conjure up!

Fabia had fed the snake last night, and it was almost time for the snake to eat again. It had no qualms about finding and eating Cryptor. After being starved by the evil wizard, the snake would enjoy its revenge. But there was no sign of Cryptor. The only thing the snake could smell nearby was a rat! That would have to do; it decided. Oddly, the rat also smelt like Cryptor. The snake hadn't seen what had happened to the evil wizard after he had rushed out of his house last night. But, it was suspicious. Was it possible that the boys, who had rescued the dragon, had somehow reduced Cryptor to this bite-sized rodent? Brilliant, if they had!

Flicking out its tongue, the snake followed the scent of the rat. There it was! Trying to hide under some roots. The rat was just out of reach, but the snake settled down to wait for it to come out. In panic, Cryptor tried to scream but it came out as a high-pitched squeal.

Hearing the noise next door, the giant badger sleepily opened its eyes. Expecting to see a rodent through the brambles, it saw the massive snake! In total shock, it shot out from under the table backwards, lost its footing and rolled across the grass. It lay on its back in a daze!

The boys looked through the brambles to see what had alarmed the giant badger and saw the snake.

'It looks like the snake has cornered Cryptor! We'd better send some food over now,' said Danny.

'There are sausages left over from lunch on the table, Mom. Can we use those, please?' Josh asked

'Of course. You'll need a spell to make a hole in both auras to get the food through' replied Fabia.

'Let's use a new ingredient,' mused Danny as he looked at Fango. 'What about dragon's fire? Fango will you aim your fiery breath at the auras while we cast a spell?'

Fango puffed up his cheeks and nodded.

As the boys chanted, 'Draco ignis!' Fango blew a long plume of fire at the spot the boys were pointing their wands at. Holes appeared in both auras.

'You must come from a family of powerful dragons,' Felix commented.

Fango threw out his chest in pride.

'Shall we shape the sausages into something the snake likes,' said Josh with a twinkle in his eyes. 'How about a large rat?'

Everyone laughed. It was a wicked idea!

Josh pointed his wand at the sausages. 'Rattus!' he chanted.

The giant badger sat up and watched in amazement as the sausages lifted off the table and moulded together until they resembled a big rat.

Pointing their wands at the snake food, the boys directed it through the hole in the auras and dropped it in front of the snake. A long serpentine tongue flicked out to test it. Then with one gulp the snake swallowed the food whole.

Everyone watched to see what the snake would do next. It settled down to wait for the evil rat to come out. It was enjoying torturing Cryptor!

Cryptor was seething amongst the roots. He would have to stay there till dark when the snake would go back to a warm fire in the dungeon.

'We won't forget you, Cryptor,' said Fabia. 'Here are the rat pellets we promised.'

Fabia tossed a bag through the holes in the auras before they closed. It landed near the tree where Cryptor was hiding. As it hit the ground, the bag split open scattering the pellets amongst the roots. Cryptor was starving. He picked one up. Scowling, he bit into it with long teeth. It was disgusting! But there was nothing else to eat. His eyes flashed red! They would all suffer for this humiliation.

The badger was still eyeing the snake and frowning. Danny walked over to it and stroked its head. 'Nothing to worry about. The snake won't reach you here.'

'We'll make sure it's never hungry again. We hope you'll still stay with us,' added Josh as he filled a large bowl with food from the table and offered it to the badger.

Reassured that all was well with the world, the badger ate heartily and decided to go back to sleep in its new den.

Felix stood admiring the snake. 'It is a superb looking snake. A very unusual one. Seems to have the characteristics of a python and a cobra. Did you notice those fangs when it opened its mouth? Venomous, no doubt. I wonder where Cryptor found it. We will try to get it back, when possible.'

'There has been so much excitement in the last twenty-four hours that I suggest we all have a quiet afternoon,' suggested Fabia. 'You only have a few more days of holiday left. You'll need to go to school as usual, and either your Dad or I will take you there. I am sure Lance will step up security in the school.'

'On the subject of school, Lance has given the order for you to return to school early. He wants everyone to work on a spell to bring the Great Warrior Wizard and his fallen Golden Army back. They will be needed in case we have to fight another war against evil. All villagers will be told at tonight's meeting,' Felix informed them.

'Can Lance really call us back to school early?' asked Danny.

'Yes, he certainly can. He is the Guardian of not just the Great Hall but of the village as well. We have never had to call for his help before, but now it is essential,' Felix replied. 'For the rest of the afternoon, I suggest you all relax while you have the chance.'

The boys turned towards Fango. The little dragon had curled up on the grass and was sound asleep. He had a lot of sleep to catch up with.

After helping Fabia to clear the table, the boys returned with their wands and practiced spells as they kept watch over Fango. Little did they suspect how much this skill would soon be needed!

The afternoon soon passed. The boys woke Fango up and led him into the kitchen for an early supper. Fango made up for the time he had been starved by Cryptor and ate everything that Fabia served him.

Felix came into the kitchen. 'I can see you all enjoyed your supper from your clean plates. I know you boys have your own bedrooms but how about sharing a bedroom with Fango while he is with us. He will feel safer with you both in the same room at night. I suggest you take the guest bedroom and change it to suit the three of you.'

'Yes,' Fabia added. 'Show Fango the bathroom you use. He will want to wash off the dust from the tunnels. We'll come up later and see you are comfortable.'

'Let's see what we can do with the guest bedroom first,' said Danny as they went upstairs.

Josh opened the fourth door at the end of the corridor.

'Very boring and dull,' said Danny. 'First of all, there are only two beds and we need three.'

The boys pointed their wands at the beds and chanted, 'Tribus lectulis!'

And suddenly there were three beds in the room!

'The middle bed is yours, Fango,' said Josh.

The little dragon looked at his bed. He had never slept in one before.

'We always have fun testing new spells on our beds. If you want a softer bed, we can cast a spell and turn it into a soft cloud or we can make it bouncy and turn it into a trampoline,' said Danny.

'Let's turn all three beds into trampolines,' said Josh. 'Fango will like that!'

Danny and Josh pointed their wands at the beds and chanted, 'Lectis ad saliendum!' Three trampolines appeared where the beds had been.

'Show us how high you can bounce, Fango,' said Danny as he and Josh jumped onto them.

The little dragon leapt onto the middle trampoline and to his astonishment shot up into the air! Each time he landed on the trampoline, he went higher and higher. The boys raised the ceiling height with a spell. Fango used his wings to go higher than the boys. He was having the time of his life!

This was going to help Fango's flying skills. They were all turning somersaults when they heard Fabia call, 'Time for bed. Please show Fango where you bathe.'

The boys grinned at each other. Theirs was no ordinary bathroom; there was even more fun to be had in there!

'This way Fango. You are in for a surprise,' laughed Danny.

He followed the boys through a door leading into a changing room. The boys took off their robes and put on swimming costumes. They opened another door and stepped into a circular room. The lights dimmed and rainbows began to appear as the air filled with tiny warm droplets of water. Suddenly, jets of water danced up and down from spouts in the floor. They were in a huge fountain!

Fango stood stock-still.

'Come on, Fango! Follow us!' laughed the boys as they ran into the jets.

Closing his mouth tight, Fango ran in after them. It was brilliant! The jets were warm and gentle at first. Then they grew stronger and stronger until they were powerful enough to lift them up into the air and toss them about. The boys whooped as they all tumbled and swirled.

Then the jets of water began to die down as the water rose and formed a perfect swimming pool. Fango looked worried.

Seeing Fango's concern, Danny said, 'It's OK, Fango. This is supposed to happen. We always finish with a swim.'

'You haven't learnt to swim yet, have you?' asked Josh.

Fango shook his head. The boys looked at each other. This was going to be fun!

Soon, they had him paddling about with his feet off the floor of the pool. Fango learnt that if he wagged his tail strongly from side to side, he could shoot forward and keep up with the boys who were excellent swimmers.

The next step was harder. 'Try swimming underwater,' encouraged Danny. 'If you hold your breath, close your mouth and open your eyes, you'll be OK.'

Fango hesitated. He didn't like the idea of this. But he trusted the boys and knew they were trying to help him. So he took a deep breath, clamped his mouth shut, and peeped out of his eyes as he sank down. He got the surprise of his life! There were colourful fish swimming around him! Fango forgot to be frightened as he watched them darting about.

Danny and Josh winked at each other. They had cast a spell and filled the pool with exotic fish. Their idea was working. Fango was underwater, running along the bottom of the pool, chasing the fish for fun until he ran out of breath. He came to the surface, took a huge gulp of air, and dived under again. He loved this game. The boys dived underwater with him, racing each other and the fish until it was time to go to bed. The spell wore off and the fish faded away as the water emptied. Then jets of warm air from the ceiling blew them dry.

Fango was enjoying every moment with the boys and was looking forward to sharing a room with them. He hadn't dared to sleep in the dungeon with the snake watching him.

They returned to the bedroom, and the boys decided to change the trampolines into comfortable rocking beds. Pointing their wands, they chanted, 'Lectulis movens!'

Three large beds on curved bases appeared where the trampolines had been. Soft feather mattresses sat on the bases. It would be like sleeping on clouds. No covers were necessary as the air was warm.

Fango sank into his mattress. It was sheer bliss.

'You're safe here with us,' said Danny. 'If you need anything, just wake us up.'

After the boys climbed into their own beds, they lay there thinking how immensely fond of Fango they already were. They were dying to see their friends' faces when they told them that they had a dragon staying with them!

Fango read their thoughts and felt happy. The misery he had been through began to fade.

All three beds started gently rocking them to sleep.

Felix and Fabia came up to say goodnight. They saw Fango was smiling. He looked comfortable and was settling in well. He was a good-natured little dragon.

They gave the boys a hug and stroked Fango under his chin. Fango sighed contentedly in his sleep. 'Sleep well and dream of wonderful places,' Fabia said.

Fango began to dream of an island far out to sea.

In their hearts, they felt sad about how badly Fango had been treated by Cryptor. They dreaded the danger this evil wizard was bringing to the village and how much all their lives might be changed. Quietly, they went downstairs to discuss how best they could protect the boys and Fango. Then it was time for Felix to go to the meeting that Lance was holding in the Village Hall.

'Guard them well until I return and update you about the meeting, Fabia.'

THE MEETING

Silently, under the cover of darkness, the villagers began gathering in the Village Hall. They spoke in hushed whispers as they waited for the Guardian to arrive. Word had spread that evil had come to the village.

They fell silent as a tall figure strode to the front of the hall and threw off a dark cloak to reveal a golden robe underneath. Taking out a wand, the Guardian pointed at the walls and doors and uttered a soundproof spell, 'Non auditus!'

Lance looked around the Hall, 'Thank you for coming at such short notice. We are in a state of High Alert. The truce that was drawn up after the Great Wizard War is being broken! An evil wizard, named Cryptor, has moved into the empty house next door to Felix and Fabia. Using this house as a base, he has been going out at night to form a new Dark Army with the intention of invading our village. I can see no other reason for Cryptor coming here but to spy on us prior to launching an attack. He has also captured a snake and a young dragon to use their ingredients for the most powerful spells!'

There were horrified gasps and low murmurs around the hall. Lance held up his hand for silence. 'For the moment, the situation is on hold. Felix, Fabia, and their sons have temporarily stopped Cryptor by taking away his powers. The boys rescued the dragon and got hold of some snakeskin and cast a reverse spell. They have also turned Cryptor into a rat. He is trapped in his garden with the snake. I will go there to capture and imprison him before the spell on him wears off.'

Lance looked at the audience. 'We must be on alert for any of Cryptor's followers. When his new Dark Army arrives, we will need everyone in the village to repel them. Our nature is not a warring one. We will act defensively and only retaliate when attacked. Although we have advanced with the times and are capable of building modern weapons that can completely wipe out the enemy, we are honourable and have never used such tactics.'

There were murmurs from the villagers. A wizard at the front stood up and said, 'Perhaps it is time we used modern warfare!'

'I realise your concerns,' Lance continued. 'But we can defeat them and force them to surrender with minimal loss of life. It is barbaric to destroy them all. We must try to make them realise that war is futile. If we find the spell that will bring back the Great Warrior Wizard and our ancestors who fell in the Great Wizard War, we can join forces with them. Then, our sheer numbers will easily overpower the enemy in the ancient form of battle they are used to.'

'So, are you saying we should use stone-age clubs?' asked an incredulous witch.

Everyone chuckled at the thought.

But Lance continued on a serious note, 'We *will* use modern defensive methods to ensure that the enemy does not reach the Dark Warlord and the evil ancestors. If they are revived with an evil spell before we can raise our own ancestors … their combined evil army will then outnumber us! We must *not* allow that to happen. The Great Hall must be made even more secure.'

Lance glanced at the front row and spotted the high tech wizard. 'Wizzo, I ask you to start creating modern defensive systems and androids to protect the Great Hall and the village.'

It was time for Lance to convince the villagers how urgently their help was needed. 'We all know that a spell to raise our ancestors will eventually wear off … but if we can raise our ancestors to fight with us, we have a good chance of a quick victory before this happens. Every one of us, including our young wizards and witches, must to try to find that spell. The younger ones will have fresh ideas. I am calling all pupils back to school early to test new spells. They are to return the day after tomorrow. Meanwhile, all the school staff must prepare the school for this.'

Cognitor, the school's Head Teacher, stood up. 'Could you tell us about the spell you cast to communicate with the Great Warrior Wizard?'

'I used seeds of large trees as the ingredients,' Lance replied. 'Seeds are the beginning of new life. The seeds from redwood, mountain ash and gum trees briefly enabled Lanzor to warn us of an uprising. Now we must try everything else we can think of to complete the spell!'

There was a heavy silence, then Lance broke it. 'While we are preparing our defences, try to give the appearance that we are still unaware of any danger. But report anything suspicious immediately.'

Looking at Felix, Lance said, 'The day after tomorrow, I will come to capture Cryptor. I must ensure the Great Hall is secure before I imprison him there. Please alert me if you suspect anything is changing next door.'

Lance turned back to the audience. 'We will all meet here again tomorrow night for further instructions. When Wizzo has the defences in place, we will base ourselves in the Great Hall for the battle that will come. Now you must return and inform your families about this meeting.'

Lance threw his dark cloak over his robe and strode out of the hall. The villagers followed in silence. It was a very dark time.

Cryptor was wide awake and shivering in the garden when he heard Felix return from the meeting. He was too cold to sleep and eyed Felix with pure hatred.

The snake had gone down the tunnel to keep warm in the dungeon. Cryptor crawled out from under the roots that had protected him from the annoying reptile. He picked up a few more rat pellets to eat. Instead of being grateful for being kept alive, he began to imagine all the terrible things he would force that interfering family to eat before he killed them. Stinging nettles mixed with monkshood flowers and deadly nightshade would do nicely. How they would writhe in agony!

Meanwhile, he must keep his ears open in case he heard any of his Deadly Wizards and Witches searching for him. He had told his followers that he had a sign on his gate with his name on it! But those boy brats had altered it. Now he had to hope that anyone looking for him would have the sense to look over the gate. He would be waiting for that moment when he planned to scratch THIS RAT IS CRYPTOR in the dirt. Then his followers would undo the spell that had been cast on him. Otherwise, he had to wait for the spell to wear off and he was losing patience …

Felix could sense the rat's evil eyes on him as he walked to his front door. He shuddered. The sooner Cryptor was dealt with the better. Going inside, Felix found Fabia waiting for him. They discussed everything that had been said in the meeting.

'So Danny and Josh have one day left before they return to school. What can we do with Fango? He has bonded well with the boys.' Fabia asked.

'I think he should go to school with them. Everyone will be trying to find the spell to revive our ancestors. Fango can provide the most powerful ingredient of all!' Felix replied. 'I will contact the Head Teacher. He will realise how useful Fango will be.'

Fabia looked thoughtful. 'I am worried that Fango might be completely overwhelmed by so many children!'

'Then we need to introduce him to some. Let's ask Ginny and Katy to spend tomorrow morning with us. I'm sure Fango will like them.'

'That's a good idea, Felix. I'll contact Gina and Tristan now and see if they can bring the girls over here, and we'll all have breakfast together. I'll make it a special treat for Fango as a welcome to his new home.'

Fabia contacted Gina via the village's private communications system that had been set up by Wizzo. It was designed to avoid detection and disguised to look like old-fashioned telephones, much to the disgust of young wizards and witches.

Gina answered the phone and happily accepted the invitation. They would be thrilled to meet a young dragon.

The next morning, all was peaceful in the boys' house. The only sound was Fango gently snoring. Little puffs of smoke rose from his nostrils. He began to dream he was being shaken and opened his eyes. All three beds were gently rocking and waking Danny and Josh up, too.

'Time to wake up,' said Fabia, who had come into the room. 'We have a special surprise for you this morning. Come down when you are ready.'

'Thanks, Mom,' said the boys.

Fango blinked his eyes. Everything here was a surprise!

When the boys had dressed, they wandered down with Fango and went into the dining area of the huge kitchen. Fango couldn't believe his eyes. There was an amazing table of treats.

Pineapples, melons, and mangos had been carved into smiley faces. Smoothies and milk shakes of every flavour could be poured at the touch of a button from a swirling crystal bowl. Jars of honey and jam sat next to waffles and pancakes. And there was the smell of freshly made bread!

'We thought we would give Fango a Breakfast Party to welcome him to our home,' said Fabia. 'Ginny and Katy are arriving with their parents any minute now. We would like Fango to meet your two closest friends.'

Just as Fabia finished speaking, the doorbell chimed. Felix went to greet their visitors and showed them into the kitchen. The girls had already been told that Fango was very young and had been rescued. They were dying to hear the full story.

Fango stood perfectly still as he looked at both girls with his huge eyes. He was busy reading the girls' thoughts.

Both girls slowly approached the little dragon and stopped before they reached him. They didn't want to frighten him and risk being scorched with flames. Little puffs of smoke from his nostrils showed he was already capable of breathing fire!

'Hello Fango,' Ginny said very gently. 'I'm Ginny and this is Katy.'

'Hello, little dragon,' whispered Katy.

Danny went up to the girls and drew them closer to Fango. 'These are our best friends, Fango.'

The little dragon already knew all about the Feisty Four from their thoughts. He nodded his head.

'Don't be afraid, girls. Fango won't bite you! He hasn't got many teeth yet,' Danny joked.

'Those two fangs are the only ones he's got so far,' Josh chuckled.

Fango closed his mouth trying to hide the objects of their attention.

'You're so cute! Can we stroke you, Fango?'

Fango wasn't sure how to respond. Dragons were *not* supposed to be cute!

Ginny slowly walked up to him and reached out her hand. She gently rubbed him between the eyes. Fango closed his eyes with pleasure.

Katy approached and tickled him under the chin. A big puff of smoke escaped from his nose. Maybe, looking cute had an upside! But he knew he wouldn't look cute for long. Fango could feel he was changing fast and his brain was working overtime. He had lost his fear as well.

Deciding that any friend of the boys was a friend of his, Fango nuzzled them both. Ginny and Katy smiled broadly. They were almost envious that the boys had a dragon. But they knew they could share him with the boys.

'Now that you've met Fango, let's all have breakfast!' Fabia waved at the table.

'Yes, tuck in everyone!' Felix added encouragingly.

Fango, still unaware of human manners, was first to the table! In the dragon world, the youngest ate first! No one minded … they were happy to see him becoming bolder. He tried everything there was. Fabia could swear he had already grown a few centimetres since last night. Even his wings looked larger! He certainly had a huge appetite. They would have to stop calling him a little dragon soon!

While everyone was still at the table, Felix spoke to the four friends. 'As you know, you are to return to school tomorrow. Lance has requested that you spend your time looking for a spell to revive our ancestors. Fango will go with you as he can provide you with the most powerful ingredient.'

'That more than makes up for having to go back early!' exclaimed Danny.

The four friends beamed at Fango. A dragon at school! Spell casting!

Felix broke into their thoughts, 'Danny and Josh will explain everything that happened here last night to the girls. Meanwhile, Fabia and I will collect seeds from our garden to test in spells.'

'Gina and I will come and help you both' said Tristan. 'The more hands the better.'

While the adults were outside, the girls listened in awed silence to the full story of Fango's rescue by the boys. Fango listened, too, and he was reading the girls' thoughts at the same time. Katy was frightened but didn't show it, so Fango came up to her and rubbed his head against hers. He knew all about the fear Cryptor could inspire.

Ginny was full of admiration for the boys'

bravery. She asked, 'Can we go outside and peep through the brambles. The snake might have come out. I am dying to see how big it is.'

'Yes. It's also time to feed it,' Danny replied. 'I'll get some sausages and you can watch us in action!'

'The best part is Fango burning holes in the auras,' said Josh. 'We'll just cast a spell to change the sausages into a shape the snake might like.'

The girls looked at Fango and he lifted his head in pride while he blew out a puff of smoke.

'Follow us. You can choose a shape,' Josh offered as he opened the door.

They went outside and peered through the bramble wall.

'No one could get through those huge thorns. It really has become a prison,' Ginny whispered.

Katy was pointing at something and trying to say something. Her face was white. This snake was even larger than she had imagined!

The other three looked in the direction she indicated. They could make out the shape of the massive reptile, sunning itself outside the entrance of the dungeon tunnel.

'I'm positive it's grown. Must be all the good sausages!' laughed Danny. 'Right what shape do you choose?'

The girls whispered together, then said, 'Frogs!'

'Fango are you ready to fire?' asked Josh

Fango stepped forward and nodded. He

took a huge breath, and his cheeks puffed out as the boys chanted, 'Draco ignis!' Then he blew out a huge flame!

The boys stared in surprise, 'That's twice as far as yesterday,' gasped Danny.

'And Fango's taller than me now! Josh exclaimed.

Both boys looked closely at Fango. Yes, he had grown and the horns on his head were developing.

'Aren't you going to feed the snake?' Ginny interrupted.

'What was it you wanted? Oh, it was frogs, wasn't it?' Danny turned and pointed his wand at the sausages Josh had brought out. 'Ranae!' he chanted.

Both boys pointed their wands at the sausages that were shaping into frogs and directed them through the holes in the auras to hover in front of the sleeping snake.

They all watched in fascination as a forked tongue flicked out. The snake lazily lifted its head and opened its mouth to display its lethal fangs. It lunged forward. In a flash the frogs were gone!

'Did you see those poison fangs?' Katy said faintly. 'Are you sure it can't escape?'

'Don't worry, Katy,' said Danny as reassuringly as he could. 'We are more concerned about Cryptor. Can anyone see where he is?'

It was Ginny who spotted him first. 'He's

over there! Near the gate! What is he doing with a stick in his mouth?' she asked in a puzzled tone.

Sure enough, there was the rat. He had spotted them and seemed to be rubbing out marks in the dirt.

'I think those are letters he's trying to rub out before we can read them! It's a message, or what's left of it. The last letters are YPTOR!' Danny gasped. 'We didn't think he had the intelligence worthy of a rat!'

'I hope none of his evil friends have seen that,' Josh said in a low voice. 'We must stop him writing messages. Let's turn the ground to rock after we get rid of those last letters.'

Before they could think of a spell, there was a loud hissing sound. The huge snake had spotted Cryptor and was slithering quickly towards him, tongue flicking as it followed the scent of its enemy! Cryptor scurried down a hole of an abandoned ants' nest in the ground. The snake just missed him! It flicked its tail in frustration. As it did so, the final letters of Cryptor's message were wiped out. The snake turned and looked at the group of friends on the other side.

Fango had also been learning the snake's language and could now read the snake's thoughts. There was a completely different side to this dangerous looking creature! Its language was colourful and amusing as it chased Cryptor around the garden.

The snake eyeballed Fango. Its message was loud and clear. *'Ain't it way past time to rescue me, too? I's bored chasin' de pesky rat. It's Cryptor, innit? I's his prisner, like yo' was! An' I's sorry fo' tryin' to eat yo'. Been starved by d' eeevil no-good wizzo' fo' so long ... jus' couldn' help it!'*

Fango looked long and hard at the snake and let the snake read his thoughts. *'When the time is right, we will rescue you, but only if you do not harm us.'*

For the first time since its capture, the snake felt hope, *'Man, yo's de man! An' dem sausage things ... keep dem comin'. Dey's deeelicious. No need to eat no one, den!'*

Fango locked eyes with the snake. *'Will you keep an eye on Cryptor, and if he writes a message again, will you rub it out? And we'll understand if you feel like a rat snack if you get a chance!'*

The snake nodded its head at Fango and went to lie on top of the hole that Cryptor had crawled down! The rat was trapped for as long as the snake lay there.

The four friends had watched Fango and the snake exchanging looks.

'Are you able to communicate with the snake, Fango?' Danny asked quietly.

Fango looked at the four friends. It was time to open his mind to them. *'Yes, I can understand the snake. And I can understand your language and thoughts, too. You are kind and good to me.'*

'Wow! This is amazing!' each of them thought. *'Fango trusts us!'*

The four friends joined hands with each other and encircled Fango. 'You're one of us, Fango! We will now be known as the Feisty Five!'

Fango looked at them in turn and thought, *'The snake could be our friend as well. It has agreed to watch Cryptor and wipe out any message he tries to write. It wants us to rescue it. If it is well fed, it won't be driven to eat any of us. Cryptor had starved it when it tried to eat me.'*

They all looked through the brambles at the massive snake as it turned its head expectantly towards them.

'We will rescue you,' Danny promised. 'As soon as Cryptor is out of the way.'

The snake nodded its head and flicked its tail from side to side.

Katy looked dubious but Fango reassured her. *'Don't worry. I will be the first to know if the snake becomes a danger to us.'*

When they heard the adults returning to the house, they joined them inside and told them about Fango communicating with the snake and with them.

'Fango must be one of the most advanced dragons to learn languages so quickly,' said Felix.

Tristan looked impressed. 'Now we need to know what type of dragon he is ... that reminds me! The girls borrowed a book on dragons recently. Have you still got it?' he asked, as he turned to the girls.

'Yes, it's at home,' Ginny replied. 'It's called *Dragons of Today*. We haven't opened it yet.'

'Perhaps, if Fango steps inside for a look, he might see dragons similar to his parents,' Tristan suggested.

'If you can recognise dragons like your parents then we will know which islands you come from. When you are strong enough, we will help you to find your home,' Fabia said gently. She was now hoping Fango's parents were alive.

Fango then surprised them all with his next thoughts. *'My parents are alive. They were able to follow me when I was captured. But we lost contact. You rescued me and have been good to me. I know from your thoughts that you are all in great danger. While I am here, I will help you before we search for my home. I know I can make your spells stronger. I have read your thoughts about the Great Wizard War and how dragons were captured by evil wizards in the past.'*

Everyone looked at Fango in astonishment. Their little dragon was far more advanced than they realised. He was thinking like an adult one!

Reading this thought, Fango puffed out his chest and tried to look fierce. He did *not* want to be called little any longer!

Smiling broadly at Fango's efforts, Gina said, 'Would the boys and Fango like to come to our house now. They can have a look in the dragon book with the girls. When they go to school tomorrow, they'll be able to tell everyone what type of dragon Fango is.'

Tristan looked meaningfully at Fabia and Felix. 'In the afternoon we could test spells at our house with the seeds we've just collected.' Tristan had the perfect way to test a spell. The adults hadn't explained that yet ... but they would that afternoon.

'That's a good idea,' said Felix. 'Take some of the snakeskin with you. Fango is able to provide the other powerful ingredient. 'I'll come and collect the boys and Fango later. It will be good for the five of them to spend time together.'

THE SEARCH FOR CRYPTOR

The Dark Army were ready to strike. Cryptor had built up the necessary numbers for his army during his last trip. He had returned to Obscura to execute the final part of his plan ... to expand his dungeon into a vast war base. He had been one day away from moving the Dark Army in. A surprise attack was now out of the question, but only Cryptor knew that.

The Deadly Wizards and Witches were all waiting in a base camp deep in Kielder Forest for Cryptor to lead them to Obscura.

The hours dragged by and the Dark Army wondered why Cryptor hadn't returned. One of the Deadly Witches pulled out a map of England. 'Cryptor said he was based in Obscura but there isn't a single place on this map by that name!' she cackled in frustration.

A Deadly Wizard named Vulpor had been left in charge during Cryptor's absence. 'We will give him one more day to come to us. If he doesn't come, then we will split up and search the whole of England for this obscure village. We will return to this base camp every third day to report any findings. Are we all agreed?'

'AGREED!' they shouted. They had waited centuries to rise up again and take over the world! They would not give up now. The long years of waiting for another war were almost over.

Cryptor had told them that Mortor and their evil ancestors were lying somewhere near Obscura. They had been busy looking for a spell to bring them back to life. Eggs of toads, lizards, spiders and centipedes in various combinations were being tested. Eggs contain new life, which was needed for the spell. When they found the final ingredient, nothing would stop them.

After a day, there was still no sign of Cryptor. Fights were breaking out amongst the evil rabble. Instead of concentrating on finding the spell for life, they started casting spells on each other!

'RIGHT YOU MISERABLE LOT!' Vulpor shouted. 'IT'S TIME FOR SEARCH PARTIES!'

Vulpor spat out orders. 'We must all appear to be ordinary people and use public transport in our search for Obscura.' He was not choosy about using modern transport. It was easier than casting spells. Vulpor had a tendency to get spells wrong, and he hid this by being an aggressive bully.

'But that will take us ages,' said Cyanor, one of the Deadly Witches. 'If we fly over villages and towns on magical creatures, it will be MUCH quicker!'

'DON'T BE STUPID! If you are seen by the inhabitants of Obscura, it would ruin Cryptor's plan of a surprise attack!' Vulpor roared. 'You won't want to face Cryptor's fury for that! He might return at any time. We have no way of knowing what has delayed him.'

Vulpor decided to keep an eye on Cyanor in case she disobeyed him. He pointed at her. 'YOU will come with ME. We will search together.'

Cyanor scowled. She had been named after the poison, cyanide, which she liked to use in her evil spells.

It was difficult to decide which of these two evil monsters was nastier. Vulpor had a preference for physical torture, like pulling teeth out! He lacked the brains to concoct potions.

They disguised themselves to look like an ordinary middle-aged couple going for a walk but their nasty sneers still made them look hideous. Their wands were hidden inside walking sticks. Cyanor also concealed a packet of cyanide in her stick. If Vulpor annoyed her enough, she would use it against him.

Leaving the forest behind them, they headed for the nearest local bus service between villages and towns to comb an area to the southwest. They asked the bus drivers and passengers if they had ever come across a village called Obscura. They were soon tired of hearing the answer, 'No.'

After a full day of searching, and as the buses were stopping for the night, they decided to book into a village inn. The village was Foxton. There was only one inn here, The Cross Keys.

They walked in and found it practically empty. Vulpor walked up to the man behind the counter and asked, 'Have you two single rooms for the night?'

'We certainly have,' he replied. 'Now the holiday season is ending, there are several available. Just one night then?'

'That depends,' said Vulpor. 'We're looking for long lost relatives. They live in a village called Obscura. Is it anywhere near here?'

'That's a coincidence! I've heard of a village being called obscure if that's what you mean. It was about a month ago. A middle-aged couple came in for lunch. He was a bad tempered man. That's why I remember him.'

'What has that got to do with Obscura?' demanded Cyanor.

'I was getting to that! The man said they'd come across this crazy village at the end of a dirt track with no signposts, and there were NO ENTRY signs everywhere!' The bartender roared with laughter. 'When he asked a couple of dimwits where the nearest car park was, they told him to try Foxton Village! He thought the village must be full of idiots! Said it was the most obscure place he'd ever seen.'

'Did the man say where this "obscure" village was?' Vulpor asked.

'No, but it can't be far, from what that couple said. I've never heard of it but I've only worked here just over a month.'

'We'll take those rooms for two nights then,' Vulpor decided.

The bartender produced a book, 'Please enter your names and addresses. Will you want breakfast in the morning?'

'We'll be up at dawn, so don't bother us with breakfast or anything else for that matter!' Vulpor growled as he wrote down their details.

The bartender took out two keys from a cabinet at the side of the bar and held them out. Two hands reached out to snatch the keys at the same time. Vulpor got there first. 'I'll decide who gets which room!' he snarled at Cyanor. She glared back venomously.

Pointing to a door, the bartender said 'Through there, up the stairs at the end of the corridor, and your rooms are on the left.' He watched them go through and shuddered. They were rude and unpleasant. He wasn't surprised they wanted separate rooms. It was obvious they couldn't stand each other! Glancing down at the book he saw Vulpor had written 'Mr & Mrs Malo, 666 Infernum Road, Silva.' He felt shivers run down his spine!

The next morning, Vulpor and Cyanor were dressed in the same clothes they had arrived in. The man who had checked them in last night was puzzled. They had no luggage and were behaving oddly. But he decided it was better to mind his own business and not ask any questions. He didn't feel safe in their presence.

As they stepped out into the street, Vulpor turned to Cyanor and growled, 'If Obscura is down a dirt road then there will be no bus service going there. We'll have to walk and follow every dirt road we come across. It'll be slow but we must be close. Do *not* do anything suspicious, Cyanor, or I will turn you into a shrew!' It was one of the few spells Vulpor could remember.

Cyanor spat back at him, 'If I don't turn you into a spider, first!'

They glared at each other in open hostility, holding their walking sticks at the ready.

'We'll sort out our differences once we find Cryptor,' Vulpor decided. He strode off and Cyanor reluctantly trotted after him, clenching her teeth.

The first dirt road they came across led them several miles towards a farm. A strong stench hit them as they rounded a bend and saw rows upon rows of pigsties! Huge pigs eyed them with interest and snorted their disgust. An ugly pair of humans who looked lost.

Vulpor and Cyanor turned on their heels

and headed away as quickly as they could from the overpowering smell. Their tempers were fraying.

The next track they followed was shorter and ended at a cottage. A few chickens were wandering around the garden with some chicks in tow.

'Let's find out if the occupants have heard of Obscura,' Vulpor suggested. He stepped onto the porch and rapped on the door with his stick. A dog barked loudly from inside. There was the sound of footsteps, and the door creaked open a fraction to reveal an elderly woman. The dog continued barking but now it was a high-pitched frantic warning bark. It could sense evil outside. The elderly woman hastily slammed the door shut and bolted it. She hurried to her phone and dialled 999. Vulpor and Cyanor could hear nothing above the sound of the dog barking. They didn't hear her calling Foxton Police Station for help.

'Let's get out of here,' muttered Cyanor. 'We're wasting our time. She won't tell us anything. But I'll kill that crazy dog first!' She raised her stick and pointed it at the door.

Vulpor knocked the stick out of her hand, 'I warn you, you stupid imbecile. NO MAGIC! That woman will alert someone if her dog drops down dead for no reason!'

He was furious and sorely tempted to carry out his threat of turning Cyanor into a shrew, but he decided to wait until they found Obscura.

Cyanor picked up her stick in angry silence. She would have her revenge, later.

They had only been walking for a few minutes when they heard a police siren heading in their direction.

'Walk on as normal!' Vulpor ordered. 'No magic!'

The police car came to a stop in front of them. There were two officers in the front. One got out and asked, 'Have you just come from the cottage down the road?'

'Yes,' Vulpor replied. 'We wanted to ask for directions but the woman who lives there wouldn't talk to us. She slammed the door on us.'

The officer looked at them carefully. 'She was badly frightened by a couple and called us. You fit her description. She has one of our retired police dogs. He warned her of a threat. I suggest you both get in the back of the car and come with us while we check she is alright.'

Under any other circumstances, Vulpor would have ordered Cyanor to turn them into slugs, as he couldn't remember this spell. Instead, he nodded to Cyanor and they both got into the police car.

They were silent as they drove off. When the car pulled up in front of the cottage, one of the officers got out. The door of the cottage opened and the old woman stepped out, followed by her dog. Sniffing the air, the dog uttered a low growl and ran to the back passenger door where Vulpor was sitting. He started barking furiously and scratching the ground. Then he ran to the officer, nudged him, gave a whine, and then ran back to the car barking frantically.

The old woman pleaded with the officer, 'Caesar is never wrong. Those people are a threat! I am sure I can sense it, too.'

The officer suspected the old woman was right as some people do have a sixth sense, and Caesar had been an outstanding police dog. Although no harm had been done, he would take the couple to the station and check them out.

'Don't worry, ma'am. We'll keep an eye on your cottage. Don't hesitate to call us again if you have any trouble. We'll leave you in peace now.' He turned and patted Caesar. 'Good boy. Stay on guard!'

The officer got back in the car. 'We'll drive you back with us,' he said to the evil pair. 'Caesar has taken exception to you, so you are safer in here. We need to ask you a few questions when we get to the station.'

'We haven't done anything wrong,' Vulpor said in a low hostile voice. 'You have no right to keep us!'

'We could charge you with trespassing on private land if you don't cooperate!' the other officer threatened.

Vulpor and Cyanor exchanged a look that said they would finally have to resort to magic, but Vulpor delayed it by saying, 'We'll gladly answer your questions in the station.' He looked anything but glad! At least a spell inside a police station would be out of sight, behind closed doors.

They pulled up inside the station yard and all four went into the building. As they were walking down the corridor, Vulpor leaned close to Cyanor and whispered, 'While I distract them, you cast a spell to make them forget why they brought us here.' Vulpor was not going to admit his feeble knowledge of spells. His method was to crush skulls, but that would lead to a huge manhunt.

The police officers lead them into an interrogation room. 'If you would both be seated, we will run through some routine questions.'

Vulpor walked in front and sat down. Noisily, he scraped the chair across the floor. From where she was standing, Cyanor pointed her walking stick with the wand hidden inside at the two officers and chanted, 'Memineris non!'

The recent memories of the two officers were wiped out. They looked blankly at each other and then at Vulpor and Cyanor. The nearest officer asked Vulpor, 'Um … how can we help you, sir?'

For the first time ever, Vulpor and Cyanor smiled at each other.

'Can you tell us the way to a village called Obscura?' the Deadly Witch asked.

'Sorry, it's not in our jurisdiction. Can't say I've heard of it, either,' the officer replied.

The other officer shook his head as well.

'We won't trouble you any further,' said Cyanor. She turned to Vulpor. 'Shall we go now, dear?'

Vulpor cringed at the endearment and caught the veiled sarcasm, 'After you, my dearest,' he responded in a cutting undertone.

Outside the station they both burst into mad cackles. They sounded like a pair of crazy hyenas!

'This Obscura is well off the beaten track if the police here are unaware of it,' Cyanor said in disgust.

'Our search has taken us up two dead ends so far. Let's try the dirt roads on the other side of Foxton tomorrow.' suggested Vulpor. 'I'm too tired to walk any further.'

Cyanor bit her tongue. Vulpor was just plain stupid. If they had been searching in the air, they wouldn't be tired. She would eliminate Vulpor once and for all when the time was right!

DRAGONS

Back at the boys' house, Tristan, Gina, and the girls thanked Felix and Fabia for the Breakfast Party. Then they left with Fango and the boys. The dragon seemed to be growing before their eyes and was now taller than Danny!

As they walked past the school on the way to the girls' house, they all glanced at Fango. He would be a sensation in school tomorrow.

A chorus of bird song greeted them when they arrived. The garden was humming with wild birds as they circled bird feeders in the trees.

Merlin was sprawled on the doorstep, sleeping off a huge meal that Gina had left for him. His days of having to catch birds to survive were over. He was welcomed and fed wherever he went. Little wonder he was a huge cat now. Merlin opened his eyes, saw Fango, and shot bolt upright with his hair on end!

'Don't worry, Merlin. Fango is now one of us!' Katy said as she picked Merlin up and cuddled him. Merlin didn't look convinced. There was no similarity there at all! But he was a good-natured cat and any friend of the girls was okay with him.

Gina turned to the Feisty Five and said, 'While I prepare a light lunch, you'll have time to look in the dragon book.'

'The book is in my bedroom,' said Ginny. 'Let's look at it there.'

Ginny led them upstairs to her room. It was not strictly a room but an area she had created by expanding space into a safari camp! She loved animals and there were holograms of small dik-diks and graceful impala wandering outside two tents and grazing on shrubs and grass. It was a peaceful scene with no predators to be seen. Ginny preferred to sleep at night! Her bed was in one of the tents, and she led them into the other one. It was set up as a study with a microscope on a table and various books scattered around it.

She picked up a book. 'Here it is! *Dragons of Today*. Are you ready to go in?' she asked.

Katy and the boys nodded. Fango looked puzzled, until he read their thoughts. Then he nodded as well.

Ginny picked up her wand and tapped the book. It grew to the size of a door and opened. One by one, they stepped inside. Fango went in first, hoping to see dragons like his parents.

The first images they saw were two Snapping

Dragons, which had mouths that shut with great force. 'Their mouths are designed to break the toughest shells,' the book informed them. 'Snapping Dragons can be found on islands east of Madagascar. They feed on whole coconuts, which they crush with blunt teeth.'

It was obvious that Fango wasn't one of these with his two front fangs!

Further on, some massive Sabre Dragons were slashing down vegetation to eat using swords that projected from their wing tips. They were the colour of steel and had icy blue eyes. Fango shook his head. They were nothing like his parents. 'These dragons can be found living on islands near Tristan da Cunha in the south Atlantic Ocean,' the book continued.

'That is so remote!' said Ginny.

'Wow! I can see Thorn Dragons over there!' Josh was pointing to some thorn trees on the horizon. 'They feed on those trees and grow thorny spikes all over their bodies!' These were brown and covered with long lethal looking spines. Nothing like Fango.

Fire Dragons, just like Fordo in the Great Hall, ambled past. They were a brilliant red and were spouting flames and smoke.

'Fire Dragons are fearless and make good defenders,' the book stated.

They looked expectantly at Fango. He was good at breathing fire. But Fango shook his head again. His parents bore no resemblance to these.

His face was beginning to fall. So far, none of these images were remotely like his parents …

They came to a large cave. 'Let's go in,' said Danny. They held their breath as they entered. The rocks all around them were gently glowing. 'This is what the rocks in our cave do!' gasped Danny.

Fango's eyes lit up! From the depths of the cave two large shapes appeared. They were green with huge green eyes and had massive fangs! As they passed the rocks, the rocks began to glow more brightly. The dragons appeared to look at Fango, and their bodies began to radiate different colours. Brilliant lights shone out of the dragons' eyes!

'Chameleon Dragons!' they gasped.

They all turned and looked at Fango in amazement! His body was radiating every colour under the sun. His eyes were shining like torches. He was one of the amazing Chameleon Dragons!

The book was telling them, 'Chameleon Dragons are the most mysterious of all the dragons. They have the incredible ability to change their body shape and colour to fit their mood. When they are young they look green and smooth. As they grow older they develop their transforming ability. If they become excited and happy, they take on rainbow colours and their eyes shine. They prefer to live in caves where the rocks respond to their moods.'

'Wow!' they all exclaimed.

'The rocks in the cavern behind the waterfall were responding to a Chameleon Dragon when Fango touched them! They knew you were one, Fango! Even though you were still very young. Chameleon Dragons must have lived there once,' Danny said in excitement.

The book interrupted them. 'When Chameleon Dragons become angry for any reason they inflate in size and turn an angry red. Fierce spikes erupt on their heads and backs and their claws become long talons. Although they are the friendliest of all the dragons, they are also the fiercest when they are provoked.

Chameleon Dragons live in the remotest part of the world. They inhabit an isolated island in the middle of the Pacific Ocean called Extrema. They guard their island well. They were the bravest dragons to fight in the Great Wizard War.'

'So, I am a Chameleon Dragon,' thought Fango. *'I owe my life to these boy wizards. I know that they will have to fight a new war against evil. Cryptor captured me to strengthen his powers and then wipe us all out with his evil army. All dragons will need to join forces with good wizards and witches again.'*

Fango was now thinking like a true Chameleon Dragon! His body began to change dramatically. He seemed larger and had turned into the ferocious dragon the book had described!

The four friends looked at him in astonishment!

'You look awesomely fierce, Fango! Those spikes on you look lethal! If we didn't know it was you, we would be terrified!' exclaimed Danny.

'We'd better tell our parents that Fango is a Chameleon Dragon. They haven't seen him changing form yet and he looks really scary now!' Josh said.

Both girls were speechless … their "cute" little dragon had vanished!

Fango was thrilled with his powerful new appearance.

Everyone stood admiring him until Ginny broke the silence, 'We can leave the book now. Mission accomplished. Fango is a top dragon!'

They stepped out of the book and Katy touched it with her wand. It closed and returned to its original size. Fango began to turn back to his familiar green colour again. But he looked larger. He was constantly growing!

Over lunch, they told Gina and Tristan everything they had discovered in the book. Gina and Tristan exchanged questioning looks. Fango read their thoughts, *'Don't worry, I'll still be a "cute" dragon with the girls!'*

Everyone laughed. Fango would always be their friendly dragon.

As soon as they had finished lunch, Tristan stood up. 'It's time to test some new spells.

Fango, will you help us by supplying some claw clippings to strengthen the spells, please?'

Fango nodded.

'I'll set up a cauldron here in the kitchen and line up samples of the seeds we collected this morning. We will take the bulk of the seeds to school tomorrow for you to continue testing there. Perkin and Quirkor will be jointly in charge of those spells. Perkin, with his knowledge of science, can advise Quirkor about some of the more hazardous ingredients. We cannot risk the whole school being blown up! Bella will assist them by keeping order.'

The four friends broke into broad grins. Having Perkin, Quirkor, and Bella in the same room was an explosive recipe anyway! This was going to be outrageously funny and entertaining!

Tristan fired the cauldron up.

'How can we know if any of our test spells work?' Danny asked. 'We don't have any of our ancestors here or at school.'

'Ah ...' Tristan paused. It was time to tell them another village secret. 'We have something just as good. A dragon that fell in the Great Wizard War!'

'We've been told that the fallen dragons lie in Fire Mountain,' said Josh.

'Yes, the majority are there. Those are the dragons that fell in battle at the same time as their riders fell. But a few wizards and witches survived whose dragons did not survive. They had grown very close to their dragons and were allowed to keep them in their state of preservation. They always hoped, that one day, a spell would be found to bring their dragons back. As you know, the descendants of the Golden Army eventually settled here in Obscura. One of my ancestors rode a Sabre Dragon that fell in the war. My family have continued to look after the Sabre Dragon here in his crystal. He lies in a vault that was built to resemble a folly. You can see it through the window.'

All heads turned to look out of the window. They could see a decorative rounded building in the garden. The girls had assumed it was just ornamental.

'You never told us that, Dad!' Katy exclaimed. She held her hand over her mouth trying to hide her shock.

'We were waiting to tell you, after you'd heard the secrets of the Great Hall. For this must also be kept secret,' Tristan explained. 'Our dragon must remain hidden from sight.'

'So, if a spell works, we'll see the Sabre Dragon come to life?' Ginny asked in a high-pitched voice.

'Indeed we will. I will open the vault door for you to see him. His name is Dragor.'

They all walked up to the folly and Tristan pulled a hidden lever. The floor in the centre slowly slid open. They all stepped forward and looked down. Lying in a massive crystal was a huge Sabre Dragon. Light reflected off his lethal looking swords at the ends of his wings. Icy blue eyes appeared to be staring straight at them. No one spoke. They were stunned!

A large drop of water fell onto the crystal, and everyone looked to see where it had come from. Another huge tear rolled out of Fango's eye. He had changed to a dark purple colour that reflected his sad mood as he viewed the Sabre Dragon.

Tristan looked at Fango. 'The fallen dragons as well as our ancestors are not technically dead. They are in a state of preservation, so don't be sad, Fango.' Turning to the others, Tristan said, 'Let's go back inside and set to work. I'll leave the vault door open while we search for a spell.'

The rest of the afternoon was spent testing different mixes of seeds with a piece of Fango's claw and a small segment of snakeskin. Nothing seemed to work.

Tristan was about to call it a day when Ginny said, 'Why don't we just strengthen Lance's spell with a piece of dragon's claw and snakeskin? We should get a partial response and hopefully a stronger one!'

'It is worth a try,' Tristan agreed. 'Though don't be disappointed if it doesn't work for long.'

The whole group stood around the cauldron. In went the mountain ash, redwood and gum tree seeds. Gina stirred the cauldron as Tristan added a piece of Fango's claw and snakeskin.

Everyone pointed their wands at the cauldron and chanted, 'Vita!'

Green smoke rose from the cauldron and drifted through the window Gina had opened. It headed straight for the folly!

They rushed outside to look at Dragor. The smoke drifted down. It slowly seeped into the crystal and curled around the Sabre Dragon. The icy blue eyes blinked and the huge head began to rise! The mighty dragon looked directly at Fango … they were communicating with each other! Fango was highly excited and he was radiating every colour imaginable. Then the Sabre Dragon lay down again and the crystal closed over him.

'I am so sorry it didn't last long,' Tristan said quietly. 'We will all keep working until we find a spell that lasts much longer!'

'Did Dragor share his thoughts with you?' Danny asked Fango.

'Yes. He wants us to call up all dragons to help stop the evil that is coming. He also wants to help when you can bring him back for longer,' Fango replied.

'I will give Dragor's message to Lance at the meeting tonight,' Tristan told them.

Just as he spoke, Felix arrived and saw them standing at the folly. He came over to join them. 'I see Tristan has shown you Dragor. He was one of the bravest Sabre Dragons. He fell when he saved Tristan's forefather.'

Felix listened quietly as they excitedly told him about the message Dragor had given them. Then they proudly told him that Fango was a Chameleon Dragon.

'I suspected you might be one, Fango. You learnt our language so quickly and you've already grown a head taller since yesterday!' Felix observed.

'As for calling up all dragons to help us,' Felix said to everyone, 'I am sure Lance will arrange that. Are you ready to go home, boys?'

Danny and Josh thanked Gina and Tristan, for having them over with Fango.

As they set off, Felix said, 'It'll be an early night, as you have school tomorrow. If there are any developments arising from the meeting tonight, your mom and I will let you know in the morning.'

Felix headed off to the meeting in the Village Hall, after the boys and Fango had gone to bed. He reported the message that Dragor had given Fango. There was a worried murmur.

Lance looked at the gathering and said in a solemn voice, 'We have to speed up our plans and call up all dragons immediately. Tonight, I will send Fordo, who guards the keep, to ask the Fire Dragons on his island to help us. To save time, some of these Fire Dragons should fly to other dragon islands and pass on our message asking for help. All dragons are to assemble in the grounds of the Great Hall. They should begin arriving tomorrow afternoon. Everyone in the village must come to the Great Hall tomorrow night, under the cover of darkness. Be prepared to stay there. We will form a new Golden Army as soon as possible.'

The room was completely silent. Lance looked at them and continued outlining his plans. 'While Fordo is away, the keep will need extra protection. I will draw up a rota of wizards to guard it until the dragons arrive. Meanwhile, please keep working on the spell to bring back our ancestors. When we find it, we will also bring back the dragons lying in Fire Mountain!'

The air was charged with excitement as everyone imagined how mighty a New Golden Army would look.

'We will continue to appear to be an unsuspecting village as long as possible. The pupils are to go back to school tomorrow as planned. It may be our best chance of finding a successful spell. With many supervised spells being tested at school, there will be less time wasted duplicating any,' Lance said. 'The school is the closest building to the Great Hall and when the dragons arrive, they will transport the pupils and staff there by evening.'

Wizzo stood up and addressed Lance. 'I have prepared the defence systems and some of the androids you requested. I will bring them over to the Great Hall tomorrow and set them up. The other androids will be ready by tomorrow night.'

'Thank you, Wizzo,' Lance replied. 'These defences will be essential. We are peaceful but we have to fight if we are attacked. We never strike first. That new Dark Army will have no concept of modern warfare, but they will understand the mighty overwhelming force we can represent fighting on dragons, even with primitive weapons to match theirs. Our destiny is not to destroy them but to force them to surrender and remember never to break another truce.'

A heavy silence descended. A second Great Wizard War was inevitable.

Early the next day, the Great Hall was bustling with urgent activity. Wizzo had arrived just after dawn to install a new defence system on the entrance. As promised, he also brought some new androids programmed to help man the Great Hall while everyone was preparing for battle.

Before coming to the Great Hall, Wizzo had programmed worker androids to build as many android replicas of the villagers as possible before nightfall. These were being assembled in the manufacturing plant back at Ye Olde Farrier's Stables.

All that Wizzo had to do now was make sure the villagers came through his defence system safely tonight. He would monitor his high tech installations himself.

Splendora arrived with a pile of golden robes she had been making flat out for the new Golden Army. She hurried back to her shop to make the robes needed for the android replicas of villagers.

Lance was in his role as the Guardian and protecting the Great Hall while Fordo was away. Helping him were the wizards he had requested at last night's meeting. As soon as Fordo returned to guard the keep, Lance was planning to go to Cryptor's house to capture him.

It was around midday when Fordo flew into the courtyard of the Great Hall. Lance came out to meet him. The Fire Dragon was breathing heavily as he reported back to Lance.

'I have called up all the Fire Dragons. The message to form a new Golden Army is being taken to other dragon islands. Bird Dragons will arrive here first. Their islands are closest and they fly fast. The Fire Dragons will follow close behind. I have hurried back to guard the keep.'

'Thank you, Fordo. Protecting the keep is the most important job now. When the other Fire Dragons arrive, have four of them surround the keep. With one dragon posted at each corner, all sides will be covered. The more protection there is, the better. It's good to have you back. I must leave you and go to the village to catch a dangerous rat. He will transform into a Deadly Wizard soon and he must be under lock and key before he does!'

Lance quickly harnessed two of his fastest unicorns and threw a steel cage into the back of a chariot. After casting spells to make the unicorns appear to be horses and his golden robe to be ordinary clothes to outsiders, he jumped on the back of the chariot and drove like the wind!

SCHOOL

While preparations were taking place in the Great Hall that day, the boys were preparing to return to school. Fango had grown overnight and was now the same height as Felix. He looked fiercer, too. The boys were delighted. He resembled a real dragon now and his wings were much larger. After breakfast, they went outside to see how well Fango could fly. Taking a deep breath, Fango extended his wings and with a leap soared into the air! He swooped over the boys and circled the house. The boys watched in admiration. As Fango flew, he started to radiate colours and his eyes shone. He was no longer helpless!

Fabia and Felix came out to watch him, and the giant badger peered enviously out of his den. Fango landed in front of them and blew out a massive fireball. They were all overwhelmed. The little dragon they had rescued bore no resemblance to this new Fango.

'*I'm still the same dragon inside, you know!*' Fango thought.

'You are the best, Fango,' Danny said.

'*I wish I could grow as fast as a dragon!*' Josh thought to himself.

Fango looked at Josh. '*I like you just as you are!*'

Josh went up and gave Fango a hug. '*Likewise!*' he thought.

Felix broke into their thoughts. 'I hardly need to escort you to school as Fango will be more than able to protect you now.'

Fango stood there proudly and addressed them, '*I am strong enough to fly one boy at a time to school. By the end of the day, I should have grown enough to manage them both at the same time.*'

Felix considered this for a moment. 'Thank you, Fango. That would save time for all of us. As a precaution, you should go under a short invisibility spell, just in case there are Cryptor's followers anywhere near. I'll cast the spell. You go first, Danny, and take some snakeskin with you. When you get to school, undo the spell on yourself and warn the children to expect Josh and Fango to emerge from an invisibility spell when they arrive. We don't want to alarm the whole school!'

Danny climbed onto Fango's back and wrapped his arms around the dragon's neck.

Felix pointed his wand at them and chanted, 'Brevis invisibilis!'

Danny and Fango vanished from sight. Felix and Josh could hear the sound of beating wings and felt a rush of air.

'I'll be back for you soon, Josh,' thought Fango.

In no time at all, Fango landed in the school playground and Danny materialised as planned. He excitedly told everyone around to expect a Chameleon Dragon to arrive with Josh. The news quickly spread and a large crowd gathered outside.

Fango flew straight back for Josh.

Felix and Josh felt a rush of air and heard Fango land. Two footprints in the soil showed Josh where Fango was standing. Josh reached out to feel Fango. The dragon crouched and Josh climbed onto his back.

Felix pointed his wand at Josh and repeated the spell, 'Brevis invisibilis!'

'Hold tight, Josh!' Fango thought. *'I'll look after them, Felix.'*

'I know you will,' Felix said. 'You're a Chameleon Dragon.'

In no time at all, Fango and Josh were circling over the school. Josh spotted Danny in the playground where the excited crowd had gathered. Cognitor, the Head Teacher, was ushering the crowd back to create a space for Fango to land. Quirkor, Bella, and Perkin were there.

As Fango flew down, the crowd fell silent as they felt a gust of wind.

Josh took out his wand and pointed it at Fango and himself and chanted, 'Visibilium!'

There were gasps from the onlookers as Josh and the Chameleon Dragon slowly appeared. Josh climbed off, as Fango began to radiate multiple colours. He was reacting happily to being the centre of so much attention.

Ginny and Katy were standing next to Danny. Fango and Josh walked up to them. Fango nuzzled the two girls in greeting. They each planted a kiss on Fango. The dragon turned bright red in embarrassment … these girls would always think he was cute! Everyone laughed and clapped. This promised to be an exciting day.

Cognitor approached the group of five friends. 'Welcome to our school, Fango. I was advised that you would help us with spells today. Please follow us inside.'

Everyone filed into the main school hall which had been turned into a large laboratory! Cauldrons were all around the perimeter, and in the middle of the hall was a huge crystal with Dragor inside it! The excitement in the room reached fever pitch when they saw the Sabre Dragon.

Cognitor turned to address them. 'Ginny and Katy's parents have brought this Sabre Dragon, called Dragor, here to help us with finding a spell to bring him back to life. This same spell should then succeed with all our ancestors and other dragons as well. I will leave Quirkor, Perkin and

Bella to organise and explain procedures to you.'

Quirkor clapped his hands for attention. On the benches in front of the cauldrons, you will find labelled packets of every type of seed that we have available. Fango is here to supply one of the most powerful ingredients there is for a spell. Danny has brought some snakeskin from an incredible snake, which is another potent ingredient. So far, the Guardian, Lance, has had partial success using redwood, mountain ash and gum tree seeds. These are amongst the tallest trees in the world. The addition of dragon's claw and snakeskin strengthened that spell yesterday when it was tested on Dragor. It is up to us to see if we can find an extra "something" that will complete the spell.'

Perkin added, 'I will supervise the addition of any poisonous plant seeds. These are used in large quantities in evil magic, but as you know, small amounts can be used in good spells. And be *extra* careful for you are using the most powerful ingredients today!'

Bella strode up to the front and twirled around. Today, she was dressed in an electric blue robe, guaranteed to catch their attention. Fango was transfixed. He stared at her with huge eyes and sparks started to fly out of them! He was totally bedazzled by this beautiful witch. Bella saw the reaction she had inspired and blew Fango a kiss! Fango bowed his head and his cheeks turned red again. Everyone giggled.

The fierce-looking Chameleon Dragon had been bowled over by Bella …

Ginny and Katy were looking crestfallen. They were in love with Fango, and Bella was stealing their dragon's heart!

Fango picked up their thoughts. He went over to Ginny and Katy and wrapped his wings around them and blew smoke rings that changed into heart shapes.

The whole hall erupted with laughter and everyone cheered.

Fango bowed, then he stepped forward and twirled around with his head thrown back, imitating Bella!

Even Quirkor and Perkin joined in with the laughter.

For the first time in her life, Bella was speechless! She had been completely upstaged by a dragon!

Now that Fango had centre stage, he faced them all and thought, *'Time for the serious stuff. We must all work together. Let the spells begin!'*

The Chameleon Dragon had taken control!

The hall burst into a hive of activity. Quirkor was confident that just one more ingredient would be needed with dragon's claw and snakeskin to strengthen the spell.

Seed after seed was tested and eliminated. Then something went horribly wrong with one spell. It was Sally's! She had selected a pod from a baobab tree to test. These giant trees had massive trunks and were known to reach a thousand years old. Sally thought the huge pod was one seed … but it contained dozens of seeds. Instead of dropping just one seed from the pod into her cauldron, she dropped the whole pod in! The cauldron began to shake and glow. Then the seeds began exploding and giving off an acidic spray. Huge holes were burnt in the floor wherever the droplets landed. The powerful ingredients had magnified the effect of the acidic pulp in the pod.

'STAND BACK FROM THE CAULDRON!' Quirkor roared! 'OPEN THE WINDOWS AND DON'T BREATHE IN THE FUMES!'

Without hesitating, Fango rushed to the cauldron and grabbed the handle in his mouth. Holding his breath he flew straight out of one of the open windows and dropped the cauldron onto one of the playing fields where it exploded like a bomb, leaving a crater in the ground.

Everyone was evacuated from the hall until the fumes cleared. They gathered outside, shocked by the thought that they might have been blown up if it hadn't been for Fango!

Bella addressed them all. 'I suggest we all have an early lunch while the androids clean up the mess in the hall.'

Sally was looking very down. Fango read her thoughts and consoled her. *'Don't be sad. No real harm has been done.'*

Sally looked at Fango and smiled. Her heart

fluttered. She had no idea that it would be possible to love a dragon!

They all trooped into the school dining room as soon as the food was ready. Fango had a helping of everything on offer. And then went back for more! He was determined to grow as fast as possible.

When everyone had finished eating, Cognitor came in. 'Firstly, I would like to thank Fango for his bravery this morning.'

There were huge cheers and applause. 'Secondly, Lance sent Fordo out last night to summon all dragons to the Great Hall. The nearest ones should start arriving this afternoon,' Cognitor continued. 'Whether or not we find the vital spell, Lance has ordered the whole school to go to the Great Hall as soon as the dragons arrive to transport you there. Today, Wizzo is arming the Great Hall with defensive systems to protect you. And lastly, all villagers will assemble in the Great Hall under the cover of darkness tonight. The intention is that by tomorrow a new Golden Army will be ready to face the evil forces that are gathering.'

There was a deathly hush while the seriousness of the situation sank in.

Quirkor stood up. 'We have only a few hours to try to find the spell before we have to leave. The androids have cleaned the assembly hall. So, let's head there and do our best.'

OBSCURA IS FOUND

The same morning that the school began its search for the spell, Vulpor and Cyanor woke up in a foul mood. They hated each other! The prospect of another day in each other's company was unbearable … it would be no surprise if one of them obliterated the other one before the end of the day!

Vulpor snarled at Cyanor, 'You'd better keep up with me while we see what's on the other side of Foxton!'

Cyanor curled her lip and simply sneered at him. He would pay dearly when the time came. She grinned grotesquely as she imagined him writhing in agony under one of her cyanide spells.

Vulpor looked at her hideous expression and blackened teeth and thought how much pleasure it would give him to pull out those ugly stumps of teeth one by one!

Without saying another word to each other,

the evil pair set off early to find Obscura. Time was running out. Vulpor wanted to return to Kielder Forest as soon as possible, to make sure the new Dark Army did not give up and go their separate ways. None of them could be trusted.

Vulpor strode out and Cyanor had to run to keep up. The first dirt road they followed looked promising, but it simply led to a small hamlet for agricultural workers. Vulpor cursed under his breath. Another complete waste of time!

An hour later, they came to a rough dirt track. There were no signposts and it was only just wide enough for a small vehicle. They followed it. To Cyanor's annoyance, it seemed to meander aimlessly for miles, at times resembling more of a ramblers' track. It appeared to be leading towards meadows and dense woods and thickets. She was utterly fed up and was about to shout that they were wasting their time again. Then she saw Vulpor, who was ahead of her, pointing his stick.

'I think I can glimpse houses behind those trees and thickets! I'll bet my life that is Obscura!' he said as he quickened his pace.

Cyanor silently accepted that bet. If it wasn't Obscura, she would cast a fatal spell and be rid of Vulpor. She gnashed her teeth and trotted after him.

It looked like an ordinary old village as they approached it. Everything seemed peaceful and quiet as they walked along the perimeter road. They passed a village school. There was a faint sound of voices coming from inside. Vulpor assumed the pupils were practising for something or other during the holidays. At least the brats weren't outside to pester them.

'Keep an eye out for Cryptor's name on a sign outside one of the houses,' hissed Vulpor. 'He said he had put one up so the Dark Army would know where to gather.'

The evil pair continued walking along the perimeter. All the gardens were well kept, but there seemed to be one with an ugly bramble hedge at the end of the road. As they came up to it, they saw a notice on the heavily chained gate, DANGER! CONDEMNED BUILDING!

'It must have been deserted a long time for those brambles to grow so big,' said Cyanor. 'Can you see over the gate?'

Vulpor strained his neck to look over and jumped back in fright. 'There's a massive snake in the garden! I've never seen anything like it.' Vulpor frowned. 'I smell a rat! We have to get in there and check it out. This could be Obscura.'

'You must be mad!' Cyanor hissed. 'Even if this is Obscura, that sign warns us of a dangerous building. If this is Cryptor's base, then where is he? That is NOT his sign! We can't go in there. That snake could be highly dangerous.'

'I have a plan,' said Vulpor. 'I'll break the chain on the gate and open it wide. We'll hide behind it, and as soon as the snake escapes, we'll dash in and slam the gate shut. Then we can investigate the building.'

Cyanor wasn't happy. 'I think we should kill the snake with a spell!'

Vulpor's eyes flashed. 'I said NO SPELLS! It would alert the village before we are ready to invade! They would smell a dead snake of that size a mile away!'

'And tell me, you MORON, how will a snake running wild in the village not alert everyone!' Cyanor spat.

This was the last straw for Vulpor. The time had come to get rid of the witch! He pointed his stick with the wand inside at Cyanor and chanted, 'Sorex!'

Cyanor's clothes fell in a heap and out from under them popped a tiny shrew!

'You'd better run and hide or the big bad snake will eat you!' Vulpor cackled. He didn't need Cyanor anymore. Obscura had been found. He hid Cyanor's clothes under some bushes and proceeded to break the chain with his bare hands.

Vulpor hauled the gate open and hid behind it. The massive snake slithered outside as fast as it could, thinking, *'I's goin'! I's goin'! Can't take no more eeevil!'*

Vulpor immediately slipped inside and slammed the gate shut. He grinned sadistically and hissed loud enough for the snake to hear. 'Lots of yummy brats and pets out there for a hungry snake!'

The snake sensed pure evil. It knew something bad had happened to one of them and didn't want to be next. It had no chance if it stayed in the garden. The moment the snake escaped, it set off to find Fango, who was able to read the snake's thoughts, and warn him. Flicking its tongue, the snake picked up the scent of Fango from hundreds of meters away and followed it. It led him to the school.

Meanwhile, Vulpor was in Cryptor's garden. A scrawny looking rat had emerged from the hole in the ground that the snake had been lying on. It was blinking at him and started jumping up and down as it squeaked excitedly.

'Another crazy creature!' Vulpor exclaimed. 'I'll exterminate it!' He swung his stick at Cryptor but the rat shot back down the hole … just before the stick crashed down.

Cryptor was fuming. He had recognised Vulpor in ordinary clothes. The idiot had tried to kill him! He would have to wait for Vulpor to enter the house, and then he could quickly scratch a message on the ground. The snake had vanished, so this message would not be rubbed out. There would be hell to pay when he changed back to a wizard!

Vulpor looked at the so-called condemned building. It looked alright to him. He assumed the tunnel under the house was for the snake. Going up to the door, Vulpor tried the handle. To his surprise, the door was unlocked. Peering in, he could see steps leading down to a vaulted dungeon. There was a cauldron on the hearth. This was looking very promising. Vulpor went down and saw bottles and vials on a table. Evil ingredients for spells! Then this *was* Cryptor's base! But where was Cryptor? He searched the rest of the house. Nothing.

Vulpor decided he would take the vials and bottles back to his base camp in the woods for the others to use in spells and potions.

As he stepped out of the house, he saw the message that Cryptor had scratched on the ground. THE RAT IS ME, CRYPTOR. But there was no sign of the rat. Cryptor was taking no chance of being flattened before Vulpor read his message.

Vulpor's heart skipped a beat in shock … he had nearly killed that rat. Cryptor would NEVER forgive him for trying to do that. Now he really HAD to kill Cryptor!

He tried to lure Cryptor out. 'I'm sorry! I didn't know it was you, Cryptor!' he whined and tried to sound convincing. 'I've been searching for you, and I'll take you back to Kielder Forest. You will lead us again when you are back in your body.'

Cryptor was trying to decide if he could trust Vulpor. Before he could make up his mind, he felt the earth vibrating. Vulpor was running overhead. Something was wrong. Hesitantly, the rat peered out of the hole and heard the sound of thundering hooves on the road outside. The gate was open, and Vulpor could be seen disappearing into some thickets on the other side of the meadow!

A chariot came to a halt in a cloud of dust outside the gate. A tall figure jumped down and slammed the gate shut!

Vulpor had also heard the approaching chariot and fled. Despite his cruel appearance, he was a coward. Vulpor would only fight or bully someone who was weaker than him. And he had abandoned Cryptor without any qualms.

The sound of the chariot had alerted Felix and Fabia. They were expecting Lance to come and capture Cryptor and came out to greet him. When they saw Lance shutting Cryptor's gate, their hearts sank. There was no sign of the snake!

Lance spoke rapidly. 'There was an evil couple here looking for Cryptor just now. I was on my way here as planned. As I passed the school I saw Cryptor's snake and Fango in the schoolyard. I knew something was wrong and stopped to find out what had happened. Fango explained how the snake had been released. I rushed here but I was too late to stop the intruders. Help me search the grounds in case Cryptor is still here.'

'Of course!' Felix said in consternation.

Fabia had gone pale with shock. They had failed to spot what had happened outside while they were testing spells.

No one knew what had happened to Cyanor. The snake had only reported hearing two evil voices on the other side of the gate. It had not seen Cyanor being turned into a shrew before Vulpor let it escape. She was now peering at them from the field across the road with tiny shrewish eyes.

Lance went to the back of his chariot and brought back a steel cage. Felix pushed the gate open for them to enter and quickly closed it behind them.

'It could take forever to find Cryptor if he is still here,' said Lance. 'I'll need a spell to locate him. He waved his wand as he chanted, 'Ubi es, Cryptor!'

Cryptor felt forced to reply. They heard squeaking sounds from the hole in the ground. So the rat hadn't managed to escape.

Lance pointed his wand directly down the hole. 'Somnus!' he chanted.

The rat fell asleep. Felix reached into the hole and pulled the rodent out. He popped it into the cage and secured the door.

Meanwhile, the shrew had crept up to the gate and was spying on them through a crack. This was her chance to turn the tables on Vulpor. If she could go to wherever they took Cryptor, she might be able to free him when she turned back into her witch's body. Vulpor would be exterminated by Cryptor for abandoning him!

On the other side of the gate, Lance was

looking worried. 'Time is running out. Our village has been located, and we can expect the new Dark Army to arrive in force quite soon. I must quickly get this evil rat under lock and key before he returns to his wizard form.'

No one noticed a tiny shrew scurrying to the chariot and climbing up one of the wheels to stow away on the undercarriage ...

As Lance drove away, Felix noticed that both auras and the ugly bramble wall were disappearing. The spells on them had begun to fade. There was no further need for them, he thought.

THE SPELL OF LIFE

A couple of hours before Cryptor had been caught and caged, the school had returned to the assembly hall after their early lunch to continue testing spells. There was a buzz of activity and hands flew as they tested one seed after another.

Suddenly, Fango froze to the spot. He was receiving thoughts from the snake!

'Yo' in der, Fango dragon? I's out here! Two eeevil wizzos came an' one let me out! Told me to eat brats, which I ain't gonna do! Warn everyone! Eeevil's in town!'

Fango rushed to the window. Below him, in the schoolyard, was the massive snake. *'Stay there. I will join you to show everyone here that you mean no harm!'* Fango replied.

Then Fango sent his thoughts to everyone in the room, *'Do NOT be afraid! There is a VERY large but friendly snake outside and it is here to help us. I am going down to show you that it is safe!'*

The whole class ran to window and gasped

when they saw the size of the reptile. And there was Fango going up to it and stroking its head! Then a figure in a golden robe hurried into the schoolyard and approached Fango. It was the Guardian! Something important and urgent was going on. The Guardian ran back to his chariot and sped out of sight!

Quirkor leaned out of the window. 'Bring the snake in. We could use some more snakeskin in our spells if it moults.'

Bella rushed to find an android cook. 'Prepare some snake food as soon as possible and bring it to us! We cannot risk a hungry snake of that size in the school!'

Fango lead the snake into the assembly hall. It was larger than they thought, and everyone cowered away except for the Feisty Five. Quirkor was having second thoughts.

'Tell dem I ain't got no appetite fo' scrawny tykes, Fango! An' it's time yo' all call me by ma name … Gnashers! 'Cause of ma big teeth!' Gnashers opened his mouth to display his massive fangs.

Everyone retreated further away!

Fango quickly reassured them all, *'Don't be afraid. This is Gnashers. He's just showing off.'*

To their relief, the android cook arrived with some food that had been shaped into a huge turkey and held the dish in front of the snake.

Gnashers opened his massive jaws and swallowed it in one gulp! *'Mmm … mmm! Deeelicious!'* thought the snake. A huge bulge appeared as the food made its way along his body. Before their eyes, the snake began to moult. His skin was too tight for the bulge! Everyone watched in fascination as a shiny new snake squeezed himself out of his old skin.

Quirkor sidled up and quietly collected the skin as it peeled off.

Ginny was standing by a window. She glanced outside to the playing fields where Fango had dropped the exploding cauldron. A huge baobab tree was now growing there! How could it have grown that fast? Could this tree be the answer to their search? She rushed over to the seed table and picked up a baobab pod. Cracking it open on the edge of the table, she took out one seed. Ginny added it to single seeds from a redwood, mountain ash and gum tree and threw them into her cauldron. Quirkor came over and gave her a piece of dragon claw and snakeskin.

Ginny threw these into the cauldron and stirred. As she pointed her wand she chanted 'Vita!'

Holding her breath, she waited … there was a faint whispering sound as a plume of multi-coloured smoke drifted out of the cauldron.

Everyone stopped what they doing and watched as it drifted towards the crystal containing Dragor. Slowly it seeped into the crystal and surrounded the Sabre Dragon. There was a mesmerised hush as Dragor's eyes began to move and focus on Fango.

Fango eyes lit up brilliantly. The dragons were communicating again!

Very slowly, the Sabre Dragon began to rise. Dragor stretched out his huge wings but kept the swords tucked in. Then he stood up!

No one moved! They were rooted to the spot as they realised that Ginny had found the spell!

Dragor looked around the room and his eyes settled on Ginny and Katy. *'You are the descendants of the wizard who fought with me in the Great Wizard War. I will help you in the coming war.'* The dragon could recall their language from the past.

Everyone had received this thought and all eyes turned to Ginny and Katy. The girls were standing there with open mouths. Fango nudged the girls towards Dragor. The two girls could barely believe this was happening. An ancient dragon to help them?

'Yes!' thought Dragor. *'But less of the ancient, please! I will protect you both!'*

The class stood transfixed until Quirkor strode up to Ginny and shook her hand. 'Well done, Ginny! You found the spell!'

Bella ran up to her, grabbed her hands and twirled her round and round in delight! Then Bella addressed everyone. 'We must all thank Ginny. We can now bring our ancestors back as well as the fallen dragons in Fire Mountain.'

The room erupted with cheers, and Ginny blushed as Dragor bowed his head to her in front of everyone.

Soon, the huge Sabre Dragon was surrounded by eager faces, all wanting a closer look at him. They tried to imagine him in battle. It was a relief to know dragons were on their side!

Perkin clapped his hands for attention. 'I have just sent a message to the Great Hall to say the spell has been found. We must prepare to go there now. Shut down all the cauldrons. Dragons from the islands are on their way. The Guardian is sending the first arrivals here to start transporting you to the Great Hall.'

There was fever pitched excitement as the cauldrons were shut down. Soon, there would be dragons everywhere!

'Look!' squealed one of the young witches as she pointed out of a window. Fast moving bird-like shapes were approaching the school. The Bird Dragons! One by one, they swooped past the windows and landed in the schoolyard.

Bella clapped her hands for attention. 'Line up in an orderly fashion. The youngest first! We already have Fango and Dragor here. Dragor has chosen to look after Ginny and Katy, so he will fly them to the Great Hall. Fango has Danny and Josh to look after.'

The boys now realised that their roles had been reversed. They were proud to have Fango look after them now! Fango read their thoughts and replied, *'I will protect you both with my life.'*

'What about Gnashers and Merlin?' asked

Katy. 'Can I take Merlin?' She was always protective of animals.

Bella could see Katy's anxiety. 'Why not! But Merlin has to want to go with you. As for the snake …' Bella hesitated.

Fango quickly interrupted her. *'I will return for Gnashers. He is one of us!'*

'Right, let's get going,' Quirkor ordered.

They filed outside and found the schoolyard full of colourful Bird Dragons. These were the smallest of the dragons. The feathers on their wings were arranged in patterns that resembled large eyes, making the dragons look dangerous when they were in the air.

The teachers helped the youngest pupils onto the dragons. One by one, the Bird Dragons took off. As each one left, another dragon arrived to take its place. Then the Fire Dragons began to arrive and a long line of dragons filled the sky as they transported their precious cargo to the safety of the Great Hall.

Katy had gone to search for Merlin. She found him in the kitchen, stretched out near a cooking range, enjoying his afternoon nap. 'Do you want to come with us, Merlin? We are all leaving,' she said as she stroked his head. His ears pricked up! There was a hive of activity going on outside. Merlin decided he wouldn't miss this for the world and followed Katy outside.

Ginny had climbed onto Dragor's back, and Merlin eyed them in surprise. Another dragon!

And the same old story of being one of us, no doubt.

'It's OK, Furball! I won't eat you! I'm the new pet in town!' Dragor thought and winked at Merlin! Everyone burst out laughing.

'When did you learn modern speech, Dragor?' Katy asked.

'Lying in my crystal and listening to you lot trying to revive me!' was the reply.

Merlin decided Dragor was OK and took a flying leap onto Ginny's lap. Katy climbed on behind Ginny.

Fango and the boys were keen to go as Fango had two trips to make. They climbed onto Fango just as Gnashers came outside and looked hopefully at them.

'I'll be back for you soon,' thought Fango.

KIELDER FOREST BASE CAMP

Vulpor headed straight back to the forest base camp after fleeing from Obscura. Time was essential! He had only just managed to escape before he was spotted by the driver of the chariot. Somehow, that driver must have known something was wrong, and the whole village would be on their guard. Obscura could no longer be attacked in secrecy. It would have to be an open full-scale war again! Vulpor didn't care about Cryptor's plight. Cryptor was as good as dead. He would be the undisputed leader from now on!

He was annoyed to see that the Deadly Wizards and Witches had become bored and were only half-heartedly trying to find a spell to bring back their ancestors. All the search parties had returned. They had begun to argue and fight amongst themselves. None of them could stand each other for long! They were intolerant, nasty individuals. One of the miserable bunch had died in a fight to the death and was lying on a bench between the cauldrons. None of their spells had brought him back. His body was becoming encased in a crystal where it would be preserved.

They barely acknowledged Vulpor's return. He glowered at them and roared at the top of his lungs, 'I HAVE FOUND OBSCURA!'

The squabbling died down. They watched as Vulpor opened a sack and took out bottles and vials. 'These are Cryptor's powerful ingredients from his house in Obscura. We will test them in our spells. Forget Cryptor! He has lost his powers and been turned into a useless rat. I will remain your new leader whether you like it or not!'

'Where is Cryptor now? And where is Cyanor? *Why* hasn't she returned with you?' demanded one of the Deadly Witches named Hecate. She used poisonous plants in her potions and she was deadlier than Cyanor. Her eyes were a virulent green. She was holding a bunch of hemlock for one of her potions in her gnarled hands. Her nails were long and sharpened at the ends. Good for gouging out eyes!

'THEY ARE BOTH AS GOOD AS DEAD!' he roared! 'I got rid of Cyanor. Now try Cryptor's ingredients in your spells, or I'll get rid of you as well! I want a spell that works before the night is over!'

Muttering under their breaths, they tested the contents of Cryptor's vials and bottles with eggs from toads, lizards, centipedes and spiders.

Hecate was using eggs from the most poisonous of these creatures in her cauldron. She added a piece of dragon claw that Vulpor had brought back. Then, from her own evil collection, she threw in a piece of snakeskin supplied by her pet adder. She began to stir the mixture.

Vulpor eyed Hecate with distaste. He would take her down a peg or two for questioning him! He strode across to her cauldron and picked up one of the potions she had made earlier. 'What rubbish is this? Something to make you uglier, if that were possible?' He laughed as he unscrewed the top and smelt the contents. Something noxious shot up his nose, and he gave a violent sneeze! Green slime spewed out of his nose and straight into Hecate's cauldron!

'You disgusting FREAK!' Hecate shouted. 'You SLIMY …' she didn't finish.

Her cauldron had begun to shake violently and then the sound of rapidly exploding firecrackers came out of it! Hecate realised a powerful force had been awakened! She pointed her wand at the cauldron and shouted, 'SURGIT!'

A foul column of dirty grey smoke rose from it and wafted over to the dead wizard. It completely enveloped him. The wizard began to cough! The whole camp watched with evil eyes. The coughing increased in intensity and the wizard sat up. The first words he uttered were, 'Where is the miserable SLIMEBALL who killed me!'

Hecate's spell had worked! More by accident than design! The final ingredient was too disgusting to contemplate.

'WE HAVE OUR SPELL!' yelled Vulpor. 'We will ride out tonight under the cover of darkness and search for our fallen ancestors and bring them back to life. They will fight with us! We will call up zilants to carry us to Obscura. These winged snakes can attack and strangle our enemy as well as deliver fatal bites. They fly silently and swiftly. We will land in the thickets outside the village. They have been left to grow wild and will provide cover for us.'

'But don't zilants have dragon characteristics as well?' Hecate interrupted. 'And we all know how dragons turned on us when we tried to use them in the first war!'

There was a strong murmur of agreement from all the Deadly Wizards and Witches.

'SILENCE! YOU STUPID COWARDS!' Vulpor yelled. 'YOU WILL DO AS I SAY! OR ELSE!' He waved his wand threateningly. 'I'll tell you why we want zilants. They are going to provide snakeskin and dragon claw clippings for our spells. We will not have enough of Cryptor's ingredients to resurrect all our Dark Army!'

They glared back at Vulpor. For once, he had a point. But they still hated him! And his sneeze had provided the missing revolting ingredient.

Vulpor continued to give orders. 'Arm yourselves with your favourite weapons for war.'

There was a scramble to assemble clubs, maces, flails and war hammers. Evil spikes protruded from the clubs and maces. The flail was the most brutal looking weapon of all. Spiked metal balls were attached to long handles by chains. That one was Vulpor's favourite. These Deadly Wizards and Witches preferred crude medieval weapons.

As the sun went down, they all gathered in a clearing. It was time to call up the zilants. They were apprehensive about these dangerous creatures. Hecate's warning words rang in their heads.

Vulpor looked at Hecate. 'You're the witch who is petrified of the zilants. Let's see you cast the spell to bring them here,' he ordered.

Hecate realised that he was either too scared to call up the zilants himself, or he was too stupid to know which spell to use. It was both!

She waved her wand in an easterly direction and screeched, 'Zilants! Veni!'

There was a deathly silence. No one dared breathe. Eventually, in the distance, loud hissing could be heard. It grew louder and louder. Massive elongated shadows appeared above the clearing. One by one, huge winged snakes dropped down and landed on legs that were scaly and had claws just like those on dragons! They looked sinister and absolutely terrifying.

The Deadly Wizards and Witches took several steps back and wondered if Vulpor had made a grave mistake. Vulpor was thinking the same thing!

Only one figure stood her ground. It was Hecate. She stared into the angry yellow eyes of the largest zilant. It had landed in front of her and appeared to be the leader of the creatures. The zilant was mesmerised by her piercing green eyes. They both appeared to go into a hypnotic trance. It was a battle of wills. The air was charged with electricity.

Vulpor had lost his tongue and was outraged that Hecate wasn't cringing in terror like everyone else. He was petrified of the zilants and waited, like the others, to see what would happen next. He hoped the zilant would swallow Hecate and save him the trouble of dealing with her!

Hecate produced a vial of one of her potions from her robe. Still keeping her eyes locked on the zilant, she unscrewed the vial and waved it under the zilant's nostrils. Its eyes glazed over and it bowed its head. Hecate had won the battle of wills by blocking the zilant's resistance. The other zilants would follow her now! She had control of their leader.

She leapt onto the zilant's back and yelled, 'I AM TAKING CHARGE! I now command the zilants, and those who will follow me as your NEW LEADER ... choose a zilant to ride!'

It was a master class in stealing power. Every one of them, except Vulpor, mounted a zilant. They had little choice. If they didn't side with Hecate, she would feed them to the zilants!

Hecate looked scornfully at Vulpor. 'I am taking you prisoner! You WILL come with MY Dark Army. You WILL complete our spells with your repulsive sneezes.' She unleashed a long whip and cracked it. It whipped through the air and wrapped around Vulpor. He was bound hand and foot by it.

Hecate turned to her new followers. 'You will obey MY orders now. When we arrive in the thickets outside Obscura, we will base ourselves there. During the night we will send out parties to try to locate our fallen ancestors.'

She glared at Vulpor. 'Now, Vulpor, direct us to Obscura or I will feed YOU to the zilants!'

Vulpor was trembling. This was the deadliest of witches who was now a ruthless leader! He croaked out directions and the Dark Army rose into the air. The wings of the zilants were soundless. Any hissing was silenced by a command from Hecate. A more evil sight could not be imagined as they swept over the treetops. Thick clouds hung over the land masking their passage through the dark.

By midnight they reached Obscura. Lights were on in some of the houses. Just as Vulpor had described, there were overgrown fields and thickets outside the village. Hecate landed her army near a thicket furthest away from the houses. The Deadly Wizards and Witches dismounted.

Hecate turned to the zilants. 'Lie low in the thickets, like snakes, until I call you,' she ordered in a low voice. Turning to the zilant she had ridden, she said, 'Keep an eye on the prisoner. If he tries to escape, eat him!'

Curious to know what Vulpor would taste like, the zilant walked up to Vulpor and opened its snake's mouth. A long forked tongue emerged and ran over Vulpor's face. He tasted obnoxious! The Zilant spat in disgust. Poison from the zilant's fangs sprayed over Vulpor and a few drops went into his eyes!

'MY EYES!' he screeched. 'They're burning! I can't see!' He was wailing his head off and staggering around until he lost his balance and knocked himself out on a tree.

Although Hecate was tempted to leave him to his fate, she needed Vulpor for the spell. So she ordered the zilant to wee on his face. The urine would wash the poison away. It was the best alternative when there was no water to hand!

The Deadly Wizards and Witches looked on in fascinated horror as the zilant did as it was told. The strong stream of urine choked Vulpor, and he woke up spluttering. He lay there soaked through and smelling viler than ever … there were no words for what went through his mind!

Hecate started to organise her followers. 'You will split up into parties of four. Each party will silently comb a different area of the village and any buildings on the outskirts. Wherever there is a large building, I want a report on what the building is for and whether it is occupied. The villagers may be together somewhere guarding our ancestors! They will not want us to find them. If you come across any rats, bring them here. One might be Cryptor! Report back to me before dawn. By then, we must know where the enemy are concentrated. If you fail to find the location of the old Dark Army, you will meet the same fate as Vulpor!'

Hecate stayed with the zilants. She needed snakeskin and dragon claw clippings from them, and she was the only one who could mesmerise them and collect these ingredients.

Vulpor watched in bitter hatred as she set about this task. He spent the night thinking of how he could take power away from her. Then Hecate would die the ugliest of deaths.

LANZOR RETURNS

Much had been happening everywhere that same day. In the early afternoon, having just missed Vulpor running out of Cryptor's garden, Lance had returned to the Great Hall with Cryptor in the cage. He knew the attack could come at any time now that Obscura had been discovered. There was much to do. The first dragons from the islands were due to arrive soon.

Wizzo was in the courtyard with his new batch of androids when Lance drew up in his chariot and picked up the caged rat. Before he discussed any plans with Wizzo, Lance cast a spell to block Cryptor's hearing. He pointed his wand at the rat and chanted, 'Audire nihil!'

'We have no time to lose, Wizzo. Fordo is fully occupied guarding the entrance to the keep from an external attack. Can you programme an android to keep an eye on Cryptor and report to us when he begins to transform back into his wizard's body? I want to question him. Could you also design a prison cell within the keep large enough to hold him?'

Wizzo was only too pleased to play such an important role. 'I'll start immediately.' He took the rat from Lance and shuddered. 'There is pure evil in those eyes! I'll use my most intelligent android, Dexter, to watch Cryptor. I left him testing the electric shield I've placed in front of the portcullis which will stop anyone using an invisibility spell from coming in when the portcullis is open. The electrical charge is enough to knock someone unconscious. Dexter turned it off when he saw you arrive.'

Lance looked impressed, 'The only other arrivals through the gates will be our villagers tonight. The shield will have to come down for them, and we must screen each one before we allow them to enter. Can you arrange that?'

'I'll set up cameras with recognition software. I have a database with every villager's details, which is presently being used to create the look-alike androids. What about security to cover entry into the fortress from the air?' Wizzo asked.

'I will have teams of dragons taking turns to circle overhead in tight formation. Nothing in the air should be able to get through even under an invisibility spell. Our huge advantage is the dragons' ability to communicate with us,' Lance replied.

No one noticed the tiny shrew coming down from the chariot's undercarriage. Cyanor was looking dishevelled and dusty from the ride. Luckily for Lance and Wizzo, her tiny shrew ears were still ringing from the thunder of the unicorns' hooves. She could not hear their voices. It took every ounce of courage in her body to scamper along the shadows and find a corner to hide in. She watched them, unnoticed.

Wizzo sent an android to find Dexter and when he arrived, they headed into the keep with the rat. Fordo was expecting them and let them pass. Lance had already warned the Fire Dragon that Wizzo had a dangerous rat to imprison there.

The tiny shrew scuttled in behind them, keeping to the shadows. Unaware of the tiny onlooker, Wizzo set about making a high security cell for Cryptor and programmed Dexter with strict instructions to watch every move he made.

As he was leaving the keep, Wizzo picked up Perkin's message from the school. He hurried to Lance. 'Great news! The spell to raise our ancestors has been found! The school has reported that a young witch named Ginny discovered it!'

'Fantastic!' Lance said with relief. 'And just in time. Send a message to the school. Tell them to prepare to come to the Great Hall as soon as dragons arrive to fly them all here.

Outside, the skies over the Great Hall had already begun to fill. Bird Dragons were arriving and landing outside the fortress walls. Lance went out to welcome the newcomers. 'Thank you for coming to help us fight a new Dark Army. You have had a long flight but I have a further request. Will you transport young wizards and witches from our village school to the inner courtyard of this fortress? They need to be protected within these walls.'

Lance picked up multiple thoughts from the dragons.

'We have come to help in any way possible.'

'Fordo has told us of the dangers we all face.'

'We will fly the young ones here for you.'

'Thank you all, again. Together, we have a better chance of defeating the new Dark Army. And I have good news! We have found a spell to revive the fallen dragons in Fire Mountain to join you for as long as our new spell lasts. Our fallen wizards and witches will also be brought back. We will have a mighty army.'

Lance repeated his greeting to the Fire Dragons when they arrived. It was important to welcome every single dragon. Each one was risking its life.

By this time, the first Bird Dragons had arrived at the school and were flying back with young wizards and witches. As soon as their charges had dismounted, the dragons returned for a second time.

Lance greeted the first arrivals from school. 'You have been brought here for your safety.

Your parents will also join us here tonight. Please come through to the great hall. Some of you older ones have been here before. I will outline our plans when everyone is here.'

Lance returned to the courtyard in time to see the older pupils arriving. Fango and Dragor were amongst the Fire Dragons. Fango was doing his best to look fierce and impressive. Lance smiled at his attempts … he was succeeding … he was a true Chameleon Dragon. By tonight all the other Chameleon Dragons from the other side of the world would also be here. He hoped Fango's parents would be among them.

Lance watched Ginny and Katy slide off the Sabre Dragon and immediately went across.

He took Ginny's hands in his. 'Thank you for finding the spell. We are all indebted to you. Your achievement will never be forgotten. Now we must put it into action here!'

With relief, Lance noticed the school staff arriving. They would supervise the school children, as he still had much to arrange. After greeting them, Lance directed them all into the great hall.

The Feisty Five and Dragor hung back. Lance read the two dragons' minds. Fango was going to return to the school to get Gnashers, and both dragons were unsure if they and the snake were welcome inside or whether they should join the other dragons outside.

With a huge smile, Lance said, 'Of course,

you are all welcome inside! Fango, Dragor *and* the snake! Hurry back with the snake, Fango. Time is running out!'

Fango sped off and as he left, more dragons arrived from further afield. The Sabre Dragons! Dragor's eyes lit up. He had so much to tell them. He flew down and was soon surrounded by excited dragons. A spell had been found which would bring back all the fallen dragons in Fire Mountain. The news spread amongst the new arrivals. The largest army of dragons ever seen would soon be assembled!

Danny, Josh, Ginny, and Katy waited outside the hall for Fango to return. Merlin was watching the dragons gathering below in bemusement. *'Don't tell me. Some more of "us"!'*

Just as the sun was setting, Fango flew in with the huge snake coiled around him. He landed with a thump, and Gnashers gratefully uncoiled himself and slithered down. Merlin and Gnashers eyeballed each other. Merlin's look said it all. *'Yeah, Yeah. I know! You're one of us!'*

When Dragor saw Fango return, he rejoined the group and they all went inside.

Quirkor and Perkin had fired up cauldrons, which were lined up in front of the crystals containing the fallen ancestors. Bella was sorting out the seeds for the spell. Cognitor was explaining to the youngest wizards and witches, who had not yet been to the Great Hall, what the crystals contained and what to expect.

An android cook arrived with a huge mound of food for the snake. Gnashers eyed it and thought, *'De food would be extra deeelicious shaped like one o' d' eeevil wizzos!'*

Fango picked up his thought. *'You're frightening enough, Gnashers, without picturing you swallowing wizards! Eat up. We need you to moult again.'*

Lance came in to observe the spell in action. Quirkor had positioned his cauldron next to Lanzor, the Great Warrior Wizard. He was going to perform the first spell to ensure it worked exactly as it had for Ginny. They all crossed their fingers. This was a spell that could change all their lives! The seeds went in first, and then Quirkor added a piece of snakeskin and a piece of dragon claw. He stirred the cauldron and chanted, 'Vita!' as he pointed his wand.

There was a hush as a plume of multicoloured smoke drifted out of the cauldron. It hovered in the air and gradually seeped into the crystal containing Lanzor. Everyone saw the Great Warrior Wizard take a deep breath as he slowly sat up and focused his gaze directly on Quirkor. Then he said, 'What took you *so* long?'

Quirkor was completely tongue-tied and fainted on the spot.

Lanzor smiled broadly. 'I was only joking. But it has been boring, lying here for centuries, waiting for someone to find a spell to get us back!'

Lance walked up to Lanzor and embraced him. They were spitting images of each other, except Lanzor looked twenty years older and his hair was whiter!

Bella was fussing over Quirkor who was sitting up and taking sips of water from a glass she was holding to his mouth. He was admiring the result of the most powerful spell he had ever cast! His name would go down in history!

While Quirkor was still in a daze, Perkin took over organising more spells to revive the other fallen ancestors! The hall was soon buzzing with activity, as Golden Wizards and Witches from the past were brought back.

Lance greeted them all. 'We do not know how long the spell that has brought you back will last. We hope it will give us time to overpower the new Dark Army while we outnumber them. We will now continue to build our army with the fallen dragons from Fire Mountain. Quirkor, you will take charge of that operation. Take as many volunteers as you need to cast the spells, and I'll ask dragons to transport you there.

Lanzor stepped to the front. 'You won't need volunteers. The wizards and witches who have just been brought back will go with Quirkor and be united with the dragons they rode in the last war.'

There was an excited murmur of agreement.

'Go well,' Lance said solemnly. 'Return as quickly as you can with all the dragons.'

Wizzo came into the hall and approached Lance, 'Reports are coming in from the villagers who are being replaced by look-alike androids. A few at a time are leaving their homes and going to Ye Olde Farrier's Stables and Yard to stay there and wait until dark, as planned. As each villager arrives, an identical android is taking their place and going to their home. These androids are programmed to act as lookouts and will act defensively if the village is targeted. They will lure any attackers into traps.'

'Excellent work, Wizzo! When it is dark, all the villagers must come to the Great Hall under invisibility spells. They have been warned that they have to materialise before they enter the fortress for your recognition software to identify them, or they will be knocked out! You will be operating the electrical defence screen at the portcullis when they arrive. No one must enter who cannot be identified.'

Lance went to the keep and inspected Cryptor's cell. It looked escape-proof. Dexter reported that all was well. Cryptor was still a rat.

'Keep vigilant, Dexter. Inform me the second he starts to transform.' Lance left feeling assured that Cryptor was contained. He could now concentrate on the final preparations for war.

From a small crack in the wall, the tiny shrew had been watching. She was now waiting for the spell on her to wear off …

THE DRAGONS UNITE

It was time for the Chameleon Dragons to arrive.

The Feisty Five had come out onto the battlements to look out for them. Fango could hardly contain himself as he scanned the dark skies with his huge eyes.

'Please, please let Fango's parents be amongst them,' they all thought as they waited in nervous expectation. The minutes seemed to stretch endlessly.

Then Fango's eyes burst into light! He had spotted large shapes approaching fast and low from the south. As they circled and prepared to land, Fango leapt off the battlements and flew towards them thinking, *'It's me, Fango!'*

Two large shapes left the low flying formation and swooped around Fango. A smaller shape followed. The dragon family were reunited! The four Chameleon Dragons were emitting brilliant rainbow colours, and their eyes blazed with happiness. They were literally spinning through the air with joy!

The four friends watched patiently as the dragons landed below and caught up with all that had happened to Fango since his capture. They were so happy for Fango and relieved to know his parents were alive.

Danny and Josh knew Fango belonged with his family, but their hearts were heavy at the thought of parting with him.

Their thoughts were suddenly interrupted by Fango. *'You're* not *getting rid of me, yet! We've a war to fight!'* Fango had come back to join them. *'My parents thank you for all you have done for me. We will all meet when this war is won. I am to protect you while my family flies into battle.'*

The friends waved to the Chameleon Dragons in acknowledgement.

Just after midnight, the dragons from Fire Mountain arrived. Each dragon had been reunited with the wizard or witch who rode it in the previous war! They caused a sensation! Everyone came out to watch and cheer as the old Golden Army swooped down. Golden robes streamed behind them as the mighty dragons descended. Lanzor, as their original leader, welcomed them. He would lead his army again! Lance would lead the new Golden Army. They would fight side by side!

CRYPTOR ESCAPES

Back in the keep, Dexter was watching Cryptor closely. He was unaware of Cyanor in the shadows behind him. The shrew had carefully watched the construction of Cryptor's high security cell. She saw Wizzo test a switch that activated a powerful force field around the rat. Anyone trying to go through that field would be repelled. It would be easy to turn the switch off when she materialised, which would be very soon.

She waited impatiently … then slowly her transformation back into a witch began. She crawled along the floor behind Dexter. The android had to be destroyed before it could warn anyone. It looked like a human, and the weakest spot was the neck. Most of the sensors would be in the head.

Cryptor spotted her behind Dexter and jumped up. Dexter was distracted by the rat's sudden movement. It gave Cyanor her chance.

She leapt on Dexter's back and ferociously

tore his head off his shoulders. With her clawed fingers she wrenched all the wiring from his head. Dexter fell down in a heap. She ripped his clothes off and put them on. In the dim light she would be mistaken for Dexter.

Cyanor looked at Cryptor whose red eyes glared back. 'I have come to rescue you,' she explained. 'Vulpor has betrayed us both. He turned me into a shrew, but his spell must be weaker than the spell that was cast on you. However, you will eventually transform, and then we need to take revenge and take control of the Dark Army again.'

She went over to the control panel where the switch for the force field was located and threw it. Low humming vibrations could be felt as the force field faded. When they stopped completely, she stepped across to the rat's cage and prised the door open. Cyanor reached in, grabbed Cryptor and shoved him into one of her pockets. This indignity alone made Cryptor loathe her.

Cyanor had to ensure they escaped from the keep without alerting anyone. The best way past the Fire Dragon would be by pretending to be Dexter. She would have to be fast.

Silently she tiptoed towards the entrance of the keep. Fordo was unaware of her as he was concentrating on possible attacks from the outside! Boldly, she walked straight to the huge door and opened a smaller man-sized hatch door at its base. Her plan worked. In the gloom, Fordo could only see Dexter's clothing and assumed Dexter had been summoned from the keep. He didn't bother to try to read Dexter's thoughts as androids were robotic machines controlled by a programme.

It was dark when Cyanor stepped outside. She could just make out the shape of the dragons on guard outside the keep. They were there to keep intruders from entering. It was safe to assume they would think anyone leaving the keep was not an intruder. As she was dressed like Dexter they might ignore her as well. She was right … the dragons were busy communicating with the dragons flying overhead on patrol. They took no notice of her!

Now to escape and get to the Dark Army. Cyanor crossed the courtyard and entered a dimly lit passageway. There were several doors on the opposite side. She listened at the first one and heard the sound of children's voices. Moving on to the second door, she put her ear against it. Hearing nothing, she slowly turned the handle. It appeared to be a storeroom. Cyanor grinned in evil delight. Stacked on some shelves were golden robes. Splendora had brought them over to clothe the new Golden Army. The Deadly Witch took Cryptor out of her pocket and discarded Dexter's clothes. She donned one of the golden robes and pulled the hood over her head. The perfect disguise!

Cyanor reached out to pick up the rat and then froze ... Cryptor had begun to shake violently. The spell on him was finally wearing off. He began to transform. Cyanor grimaced. He was hideous. Trying to avert her eyes, she quickly offered him one of the golden robes.

Cursing under his breath, Cryptor snatched the robe from her. 'Don't you dare stare at me, you obnoxious witch!' Not one word of thanks went to Cyanor for rescuing him. Gratitude was a weakness in his eyes.

She sneered back at him, 'Look at who is calling who obnoxious!' She began to wonder why she had bothered to rescue Cryptor. He was nastier than Vulpor. But she had been foolish enough to try, and they still had to escape.

They stepped out of the storeroom and quietly made their way down the passageway towards the front of the fortress. Neither of them had wands, and they needed to get through the main entrance.

From the shadows, they observed villagers arriving under the portcullis while Wizzo was identifying them. Everyone was being checked coming in.

Wizzo was now exhausted. He had been working non-stop. Many wizards who had been revived were now going outside to tend to their dragons. Wizzo set up his recognition software to scan all the faces leaving the fortress, so they could be identified when they re-entered. It was assumed that only genuine Golden Wizards and Witches were inside the fortress. Wizzo had been ordered to allow them passage in and out! As Cryptor and Cyanor approached wearing golden robes, Wizzo simply asked them to look at the cameras. He thought that these two were from Lanzor's Golden Army. The recognition software recorded them. Without a second thought Wizzo switched off the electric shield and let them through.

The Deadly Wizard and Witch walked over the drawbridge and hurried away. Now all they had to do was find the new Dark Army.

THE ATTACK ON OBSCURA

The search parties that Hecate had sent out to comb Obscura during the night were reporting back to her. They had all observed normal activity in every house they had spied on. Larger buildings within the village had no signs of gatherings or activity in them. None of Hecate's spies suspected they had been observing androids that had taken the villagers' places in their homes.

There was a commotion when the last search party returned. They had two captives in golden robes who were heavily chained and gagged. 'We found these two wandering around in the shadows. Didn't give them a chance to speak in case they cast one of their spells on us!'

Hecate strode up to them and threw off the captives' hoods. She went pale. 'It's Cryptor and Cyanor! You FOOLS! Unchain them! NOW!' She was furious but for all the wrong reasons.

Cryptor was their original leader. Her followers would desert her for him!

Cryptor was in a towering rage by the time he was unchained. He grabbed the nearest wand he could find and changed his captors into scorpions! 'HIDE! Before I stamp you into the dust!' he screeched.

They scurried away and disappeared under some leaves next to a familiar figure. It was Vulpor! And he was heavily bound in the coils of a whip. Hecate's whip! Cryptor's eyes flared at the sight! Vulpor had been Cryptor's second-in-command and Cryptor realised that Hecate must have seized power from Vulpor. He didn't care why Vulpor was now Hecate's prisoner. All Cryptor wanted was revenge!

He shouted, 'VULPOR! YOU LEFT ME TO DIE, YOU COWARD! It's time for YOU to die!'

Hecate had to stop Cryptor! Vulpor was vital for their evil spell. She screeched at the top of her voice, 'STOP! DON'T KILL HIM! We need Vulpor for the spell to bring back our ancestors! KILL HIM LATER!'

Cryptor seethed with frustration as Hecate explained everything. It was then that Cryptor noticed the zilant guarding Vulpor in the shadows. The zilant's eyes glowed with malice as it looked at Cryptor. It was under Hecate's spell, and no one else could control it. Cryptor shuddered. 'You expect us to ride those creatures, Hecate? You must be mad!'

Hecate now realised that she could use the zilants to seize power from Cryptor as well. He was afraid of them. But she would bide her time. The Deadly Wizards and Witches were still pleased to see their original leader return.

'The zilants listen to me, Cryptor. They should be as powerful as any dragon on the battlefield.'

Cryptor could see no better alternative. The zilants were already here anyway. He also needed to reassert his authority on this squabbling Dark Army.

'I have just escaped from a fortress on the outskirts of Obscura. A mighty Golden Army is gathering there. They have called up dragons in huge numbers. We have to find our ancestors and bring them back or we will be badly outnumbered. The fortress is being protected and heavily guarded by dragons, so this must be where they lie. We need hostages to bargain our way into the fortress. I overheard the idiots, who just dragged us here in chains, say there were villagers in Obscura. They will make perfect hostages. At dawn we will swoop into the village on zilants and take captives.'

Hecate had been wondering why the villagers were still in Obscura and not sheltering in this fortress. She smelt a trap. If Cryptor fell into the trap, she could take power again. She smiled cruelly and walked over to her zilant. It lowered its head as she approached. It was avoiding eye contact with the heinous witch. She whispered in its ear, 'Be ready to lead all the zilants in the morning. You will obey *me*. No one else, you hear!'

The zilant hissed in disgust. It loathed this evil witch who had robbed it of its free will.

During the night, the usual squabbles broke out amongst the Dark Army. Cryptor spent his time threatening the disorderly bunch. They were their own worst enemy! When they had nothing to do, they turned on each other. But when they had one mutual enemy to face, they were deadly!

Cyanor went up to Hecate. They were by far the most cunning of the witches. Cryptor watched them whispering to each other. He was suspicious. They smelt of trouble and he ought to get rid of them. But Hecate controlled the zilants, and the Dark Army needed these to combat those dragons! He was seething inside. He couldn't get rid of Vulpor either! And he hadn't yet managed to eliminate those brats who had messed up his plans in the first place. Those brats had caused him endless trouble, and they would pay for it!

When dawn finally came, Cryptor checked that they had enough ingredients for the spell to revive their ancestors. Hecate had already collected snakeskin and dragon claws. There were vials with sufficient eggs. All they needed was the foul ingredient from Vulpor. When

Cryptor asked for volunteers to make Vulpor sneeze and collect the disgusting slime from his nose, no one stepped forward. That was too gross … even for them! With a malicious smile he turned to Hecate and Cyanor. 'You two can have the pleasure!'

The two Deadly Witches looked at each and nodded. But their nods were secretly sealing an agreement they had made during the night to overthrow Cryptor when the time was right! *That* would give them great pleasure!

Cryptor felt pleased with himself for putting those two witches in their place.

He wasn't pleased for long. A heavy fog rolled across the whole area reducing visibility to a few feet! Cryptor was livid. 'Does anyone know a spell to get rid of fog?'

There was no response. All their spells were designed to create havoc.

Cryptor glared at them. 'Useless thugs!' He paused to think. 'This fog changes how we attack the village! The zilants are useless in this. They won't see where to land! We will carry out sneak attacks on foot instead.'

He proceeded to order two dozen small groups of the blood-thirstiest wizards and witches to target as many houses as possible and capture hostages. He had no conscience about using the hostages as human shields as well as threatening to kill them in order to gain access to the fortress.

Hecate had been listening with glee. Cryptor was too stupid to see that he was walking into a trap!

The unruly mob could hardly wait to get going. Action at last! Each group picked their preferred weapons of clubs, maces, flails and war hammers and melted into the thick fog in the direction of the village. The others looked on enviously. There were rebellious mutters amongst the majority who had been left behind. They couldn't understand why they couldn't all go. Hecate heard their complaints. This suited her perfectly. It would be easy to turn them against Cryptor and lead them again!

The first house in the village to be attacked by one of the groups was Ginny and Katy's! The look-alike androids standing in for Gina and Tristan were waiting. They had detected four thermal images approaching at ground level. Wizzo had programmed them to lure any attackers towards the aquarium. The androids stepped out, making sure they were seen by the group of Deadly Wizards. Then they turned and ran to the aquarium. The Deadly Wizards charged after them, swinging their flails and war hammers. The androids veered sharply, ran into the chamber where the glass submarine was docked and entered it!

The Deadly Wizards jumped in after them. One of them yelled, 'We've got you cornered! Give yourselves up!'

Ignoring them, one of the androids hit a control button. The chamber doors closed, but the sub doors didn't! Water poured into the chamber and rushed into the sub, sweeping the Deadly Wizards off their feet. The android pressed another button and the sub nosed up the water tunnel into the shark tank with the sub door still open! Huge shadowy forms swam up to investigate …

The Deadly Wizards tried to point their wands and scream a death spell, but their mouths filled with water. With horror, they watched a tiger shark swim into the sub. It opened its mouth and grabbed the arm of one of the wizards, who tried to hit it with a war hammer. The others attempted to swing their weapons at the shark, but they were useless in water! All four died of fright or drowning!

The shark spat out the arm in disgust. It had never tasted anything so revolting! Detecting nothing edible, the shark glided out of the sub.

The androids reversed the sub back into the chamber and waited for further orders.

All over Obscura, traps had been set by the androids. A number of Deadly Wizards and Witches never made it back! A few groups got lost in the fog and decided to desert the Dark Army. Much as they enjoyed fighting, their fear of zilants was greater. Some managed to escape the androids and returned to the base. Only one group succeeded in bringing back a hostage. They proudly dragged their captive in front of Cryptor. But something was wrong! The hostage was jerking and twitching. Then one of its eyes fell out and dangled from its socket by a wire! Cryptor strode up to it and stared at it in shock as the truth dawned.

Hecate was thrilled! She knew it had been a trap! It was time for her to seize power again!

Shrieking at the top of her voice, she addressed the remaining Dark Army. 'CRYPTOR HAS LOST THE FIRST BATTLE! He is worse than useless! If you follow him, you will lose the war! I am taking power again with the zilants at my command!' Taking out another whip, Hecate cracked it loudly, and it curled around Cryptor before he could reach for his wand and retaliate.

'We must bring back all our ancestors. We need them now that our numbers have been depleted by Cryptor's stupidity,' she ranted. 'Cyanor knows the fortress and will sneak in with the ingredients and cast the spell. The Golden Army will be expecting a major attack and not worrying about a single Deadly Witch!'

Cyanor walked up to Cryptor and sneered, 'I wasted my time saving you! But at least I learnt my way around the fortress. Those idiots manning the main entrance thought we were members of the Golden Army when we were scanned and recorded going out. I can simply walk back in wearing the stolen golden robe. You forgot that! Instead, you had some stupid plan about using hostages to get in! IMBECILE!'

Before Cryptor could reply, she gagged him. She went up to Vulpor and gagged him as well. Cryptor and Vulpor were trussed up next to each other and left for the zilant to guard.

THE DEADLY
ANCESTORS STRIKE

Inside the fortress, the villagers had spent some time with their children during the night, trying to reassure them that all would end well. Everyone was given golden robes to wear. It would be essential to identify them if the battle spread into the fortress.

By the morning final preparations for war were complete. The new and the old Golden Armies were ready.

The new Golden Army was made up of villagers who would go to war on the dragons from the islands. At dawn they went out to meet their dragons. This time, the Golden Witches would cast spells from the air, high above the war zone, and would ride the fast and highly manoeuvrable Bird Dragons. These dragons could quickly avoid evil spells being directed at them. The Golden Wizards would fly in low on larger fighting dragons that would also join in the battle.

The old Golden Army had assembled in its original formation. War was familiar to them.

It was a stunning sight! A sea of gold on magnificent dragons! The dragons raised their heads proudly and plumes of smoke rose from their nostrils as they snorted in anticipation.

The two leaders faced their Golden Armies. The Guardian was mounted on a Chameleon Dragon. Lance had asked Fango's father to be his dragon in combat. The Great Warrior Wizard was astride Zorgo, his great friend and dragon leader during the first Great Wizard War.

Their war plan had been drawn up. They were expecting the Dark Army to use magical creatures to fly into the village to mount a savage attack. While the Dark Army would be fully occupied fighting the androids, the Golden Armies would split and fly in on either side of the village. Their enemy would be trapped in a pincer movement and outnumbered. The fight should be swift with the least loss of life. The Dark Army would be forced to surrender.

That is exactly what would have happened! But the dense fog changed everything! Wizzo was in constant communication with the androids in the village. Their first alert was that a heavy fog had come down. Not long after that some androids were reporting that thermal images were approaching the houses they were stationed in. It wasn't a mass attack from the air.

The Dark Army was secretively approaching on foot and in small groups!

Wizzo quickly relayed the reports to Lance and Lanzor. Lance addressed the Golden Armies. 'The situation has changed. A fog has descended on the village. Small groups of Deadly Wizards are carrying out stealth attacks on Obscura. They are on foot and targeting the houses manned by our androids. It is a small-scale attack and the bulk of the Dark Army must be hiding nearby. We won't be able to execute an aerial attack in fog. However, our androids should be able to cope without our help as they are facing small groups. We will await the outcome of these skirmishes and draw up new plans. Meanwhile, I see the fog is rolling towards us!'

The whole situation was about to be completely changed again for walking towards the fortress and hidden by the incoming fog was Cyanor. She reached the fortress and crossed the drawbridge. She was wearing the stolen golden robe and had secreted vials of ingredients for the deadly spell under it as well as some wands. As she reached the portcullis, Wizzo turned on the recognition software to scan her. His attention was diverted as he monitored the androids fighting in the village. Cyanor had been recorded leaving, and she was recognised and automatically allowed re-entry. The electric field was deactivated, and she quickly entered the fortress. Then she pulled her hood over her head again and melted into the shadows.

Now she needed to get into the keep. There would be no reason to suspect a Golden Witch who was already within the fortress.

Had they discovered that Cryptor was missing and that Dexter had been destroyed? The dragon had seen her leaving dressed as Dexter but that was only late last night. She would tell the dragon that she had been sent to check that all was well within the keep. That should work whether or not they knew Cryptor had gone.

Boldly, Cyanor stepped through the hatch door and into the keep. The dragons outside were communicating with Fordo and bringing him up to date with events outside.

Cyanor quickly said, 'I have been sent to see all is well inside the keep.' She walked briskly past Fordo. The large dragon glanced at her and continued picking up the other dragons' thoughts. He saw no reason to suspect a Golden Witch. Believing Dexter had left, Fordo had regularly checked for evil thoughts coming from the room where Cryptor had been. As there was nothing, he presumed Cryptor was asleep, and this witch had been sent to double check.

So far, Cyanor had been lucky due to her brazenness. But there was no time to lose! She looked around. Their fallen ancestors must be here somewhere. In the dim light she saw a heavily bolted door. She ran to it, slid the bolts open, and stepped into a chamber where a figure was lying in a crystal. Cyanor leaned over to look and found herself staring straight into the eyes of Mortor, the Dark Warlord himself! Her heart sank! He looked like an even deadlier version of Cryptor! If she revived him then she and Hecate would never rule! Closing her eyes, she decided she would look for all the other evil ancestors and revive them. They must be somewhere else in the keep, and she would pretend that she hadn't found the Dark Warlord. There was a good chance she would get away with her plan.

She left the chamber and bolted the door again. There were two other doors in the wall, and the middle door led to the room where Cryptor had been imprisoned. She opened the third door. There were stone stairs leading down to a massive vault. This looked promising! Cyanor closed the door behind her and ran down using her wand as a torch to light up the area.

Row upon row of evil ancestors lay there. She had found them! Now she had to revive them without the dragon hearing her. She pointed her wand at the door upstairs and whispered, 'Non sonus'. Then she threw off the golden robe. There was a risk that the ancestors would mistake her for a Golden Witch when she revived them and try to overpower her.

To speed things up, she would have to use more than one cauldron. Pointing her wand in front of the first ten crystals, she chanted, 'Decem ollas!' Ten cauldrons appeared and Cyanor fired them up. From her robe she took out the precious vials of ingredients. She ran to each cauldron throwing in eggs from toads, lizards, centipedes and spiders. Then she added a piece of zilant's claw and snakeskin. Finally, she added a drop of Vulpor's foul slime. Stirring each cauldron in turn, she pointed her wand and chanted, 'Surgit!'

The cauldrons began to glow and emit filthy grey smoke which curled over the crystals next to them. The smoke oozed over the evil ancestors. Slowly they began to rise, coughing and spluttering.

'Where is the Dark Warlord?' demanded one. 'We have waited too long to be brought back!'

Cyanor immediately took command, 'The Dark Lord is hidden elsewhere! There is no time to search for him! I have come from a new Dark Army to rescue you. Help me to revive all the others lying here. You are needed in another war against a huge Golden Army. We are in a vault below their fortress. Above us, this enemy army is massing. Hurry! Drag these cauldrons to the next ten crystals, and help me with the spell.' She handed out the wands that she had smuggled in.

Evil charged through their veins and glowed in their eyes. Another war! A chance for revenge!

They couldn't move fast enough to help Cyanor. She didn't notice one of the wizards watching her suspiciously.

Within an hour, the original Dark Army had been revived.

Cyanor outlined her plan. 'If we try to attack from here, we are heavily outnumbered with only a few wands between us. We need to escape and join forces with the new Dark Army. They are hiding outside these grounds and are waiting for us. We will not be able to leave this fortress undetected. The modern wizards guarding this place have set up a shield on the main entrance that will stop us … even if we use invisibility spells! We have no spells to disable modern contraptions.'

'Let's call up warhorses to fly us out!' growled one of the Deadly Wizards.

'No!' Cyanor said emphatically. 'There is the largest army of dragons you've ever seen here. They are circling overhead and are all over the grounds. We will take a hostage! There are young wizards and witches in the fortress. I heard them in a room that I can reach from one of the passageways. I will storm the room and grab one. We all know those pathetic good wizards and witches would never let one of their children die in our hands! They'll do anything to keep their precious one alive and allow us to leave!'

One of the grotesque Dark Witches cackled, 'Such a stupid lot. Not like us. We wouldn't care if they took one of our brats hostage!'

Cyanor snorted and looked at the evil gathering. 'Wait here until I return for you. I cast a soundproof spell on the door because there is a Fire Dragon upstairs guarding this keep. So stay on this side of the door. I need that hostage before I can get you all past the dragon. I am going out disguised as a Golden Witch. Do NOT kill me when I return dressed as one!' With that, she threw the golden robe on again.

There were dark mutterings amongst the evil ancestors. They hated taking orders, but this witch had revived them and knew how to get them out to fight another war.

No one noticed a Deadly Wizard slip away into the shadows at the back of the vault. It was the wizard who had eyed Cyanor suspiciously, and he had one of the wands she had handed out. Inside his robe, he had hidden some ingredients for the evil spell of life. He didn't believe a word Cyanor had said about not finding Mortor. He would to bide his time and find the Dark Warlord. From the shadows he watched Cyanor go up the steps and through the door.

She quickly strode past Dragor saying, 'I'll report that everything is in order.'

Dragor was still tuned in to everything that was happening outside. If an attack came, it would be from the air, the other dragons were telling him. He barely noticed Cyanor. And there was no reason for him to read her thoughts.

Cyanor entered the main building and

headed to where she had heard young voices. She listened at the door. The brats were definitely in there. Without wasting any more time, Cyanor launched herself through the door with her wand at the ready.

Inside the room, Bella was holding a history lesson about the first Great Wizard War. It had been decided that lessons should continue in the fortress.

Next door, in the main hall, Fango and Dragor were helping Gnashers to learn the wizards' and witches' language. Gnashers found this complex language kept giving him a headache. He wished they could use a simple lingo like his own.

Fango could hear the lesson next door. They were enjoying themselves. Bella had everyone enthralled. She looked riveting in a golden gown as she whirled around in her usual fashion. The pupils felt transported into the world Bella was describing. Their golden robes made them feel like members of the Golden Army.

Suddenly the door at the back of the room flew open with a crash. A witch dressed in a golden robe burst in! Their first thought was that this witch had come to warn them about something.

As soon as Fango picked up this thought, he charged into the classroom. Fango saw Cyanor at the back and read her thoughts! He warned them. *'Keep away from that witch behind you. She is evil! She's dressed like you!'*

Fango wanted to incinerate her with a fireball but there were pupils in the way. As he started to run towards the witch, he saw a hideous gnarled hand reach out and grab one of the pupils. It was Katy!

Dragor had followed Fango into the room. When he saw Katy in danger, he opened his wings with the lethal sabres on them and rushed forward to attack the witch.

The Deadly Witch jabbed her wand into Katy's neck and shouted, 'STOP! OR SHE DIES!'

Fango and Dragor stopped in their tracks. Fango sent his thoughts to everyone except Cyanor, *'Stand still, everyone! This witch means what she said. We will rescue Katy when it is safe to do so! I am not allowing the evil witch to read my mind. We can communicate without her knowing!'*

Cyanor said threateningly, 'I am taking this brat hostage. If anyone stops me, the brat dies!'

To everyone's surprise, Bella strode up to the witch and mustering up her courage said, 'Take me hostage; instead. Let the girl go!'

'I'm not stupid! You idiots think that a child's life is more valuable than your own!' Cyanor spat.

'Then take us both!' Bella persisted. She wanted to be on hand to help Katy escape if a chance presented itself.

The Deadly Witch considered the pros and cons of this. Two hostages were better than one. And this one was stupid enough to volunteer.

The Dark Army would enjoy torturing her for information. She was bound to know more than the brat about any war plans!

Fango looked at Bella and Katy and thought, *'Keep in contact with Dragor and me by thought. Describe your surroundings and everything that happens. We will follow unnoticed. We WILL rescue you!'*

Tears were streaming down Katy's face. Ginny was crying as well. She took a step forward and was going to tell the Deadly Witch to take her instead of Katy. Danny and Josh knew exactly what she was about to do and held her back. Fango read Ginny's mind and warned her. *'Don't do it! The evil witch will take you as well as Katy and Bella. I have read her vile mind. I promise I will bring Katy back safely. Trust me, Ginny.'*

'I trust you, Fango!' Ginny thought as she sobbed her heart out.

Danny and Josh nodded at each other and put their arms around Ginny while Danny quietly whispered in her ear, 'We three will go with Fango and Dragor and help to rescue Katy and Bella.'

Bella was now by Katy's side and holding her hand. Cyanor pushed them to the back door and into the passage, viciously jabbing her wand into Bella's spine as they stepped into the courtyard.

Cyanor shrieked at the dragons outside the keep. 'Make a single move and these hostages DIE!'

She pushed Katy and Bella towards the door of the keep. The dragons outside looked on helplessly. They could not incinerate the witch without killing the hostages as well.

Simultaneously, the dragons began to send out warning thoughts to everyone.

Fordo was warned that they were about to enter the keep. He stared at Cyanor in frustration as they stepped through the door. He let Katy and Bella read his thoughts. *'If you can manage to step away from the witch, I might be able to fry her.'*

But Cyanor was well aware of this danger and used Katy as a shield.

Lance and Lanzor picked up all the warning thoughts. They immediately issued instructions that the safety of the hostages must come first. The armies were put on full alert while the two leaders hurried to the fortress entrance to assess the situation.

It was then that Fordo sent Lance and Lanzor the worst news. *'The evil witch has entered the keep with the two hostages and is now emerging with hordes of evil ancestors. They have been revived!'*

Cyanor still had Katy as a human shield with Bella next to her. The original Dark Army were close behind. Several evil wands were pointing at the hostages from behind as they marched towards the portcullis.

Lance and Lanzor stood their ground in front of the horde. It would be highly dangerous to try to cast spells on the evil crowd. There was a high risk an evil death spell could hit a hostage before they could stop it. They could see five wands pointed right at Katy and there could be more.

'Spells are not possible,' Lance uttered under his breath. He clenched his fists in anger at the sight.

They watched in horror as Cyanor thrust her wand into Katy's cheek.

'LET US PASS OR SHE DIES! NOW!' Cyanor screeched.

'STOP!' Lance yelled. 'We will allow you leave, but I warn you ... if you touch a single hair on their heads, you will pay dearly! I promise we will hunt every single one of you down!' His voice was pure ice and steel.

The two leaders stepped aside.

Katy and Bella were as white as sheets and Katy appeared to be in a state of shock.

Cyanor sneered at the two leaders, 'And I warn YOU ... if we see any of you, or your dragons, or any of your stupid contraptions above us or following us, these hostages will die a horrible death!'

Lance turned to Wizzo who was shaking in disbelief. 'Let them pass!'

Wizzo watched in crestfallen anguish as they filed past him. His defences had been breached. Somehow his security system had failed. And he didn't know how it had happened.

Lanzor went to tell the armies outside to stay

where they were. They, too, watched helplessly as the evil rabble marched into the distance.

The dragons were seething with anger. Only cowards hid behind hostages! Jets of smoke escaped their nostrils as they snorted with disdain. When the next battle commenced, they would unleash their full fury on the enemy.

Lance was about to join Lanzor and draw up rescue plans when he heard rapid footsteps approaching from behind. He was startled to see Danny, Josh and Ginny with Fango and Dragor running behind them! The children were meant to be in the main hall where they could be best protected.

Before Lance could order them back, Danny spoke. 'Fango and Dragor are communicating with Katy and Bella who are describing the route the Dark Army are taking. If we stay out of sight, on the trail being described, we will know the location of the Dark Army when they stop. We might even be able to rescue Katy and Bella. Our dragons will read the minds of the Deadly Wizards and Witches if we can get close enough without being seen and find out their plans. Then we'll try to send a message to you!'

Fango interrupted, *'Their thoughts are getting weaker. We need to leave now before contact is lost!'*

Lance made a quick decision. 'Go safely and stay on foot! Don't use spells as the enemy have several wands pointing at Katy. Promise *not* to risk your lives. At the first sign of danger, turn back. If there is no chance to rescue Bella and Katy, hurry back with their location, and we will try another rescue plan. Meanwhile, the Golden Armies will remain on full alert.'

Turning to Wizzo, Lance said, 'Let these brave ones pass and look out for their return. And instruct the androids in the village to keep a lookout for anything unusual.'

They all heard an annoyed hissing sound behind them. It was Gnashers, slithering as fast as he could towards them. And they could understand his thoughts!

'Wait fo' meeee! Yo' NOT leavin' me out! I can follo' any scent fo' miles! Specially de smelly eeevil wizzos!'

'Let the snake pass as well, Wizzo. Gnashers is now a member of the Golden Army!' Lance declared.

Gnashers proudly spread out his cobra's hood and followed them out of the fortress. Progress was slow as the Dark Army was on foot. Fango and Dragor took it in turns to lead the group along the route that Katy and Bella were describing in their thoughts. On leaving the fortress, the Dark Army had turned left and breached the wall surrounding the grounds. They were walking through meadows and not following any road or path. There was little cover in some places and the group following in their footsteps had to hang back in case they were seen. The dragons were then out of range of Katy and Bella's thoughts.

This is where Gnashers took over. Flicking his tongue in and out, the sensors on his tongue quickly picked up the trail again. *'An' yo' lot nearly left me beeehind!'* He couldn't help bragging. *'An' now I's a Gold'n Warrrer Snake!'*

Fango and Dragor rolled their eyes, but they let Gnashers have his moment of glory.

'We seem to be heading in a semi-circular direction to the other side of Obscura,' Ginny observed. She was determined to find her sister.

Fango was striding proudly with Danny and Josh on his back. Both boys felt like Golden Warrior Wizards on their Chameleon Dragon. Ginny was riding Dragor and he was determined nothing would happen to her. He was berating himself for failing to protect Katy. He would give his life to get her back!

Fango broke into their thoughts, *'Katy and Bella are now entering thickets with their captors. An evil witch has come out to meet them and is now leading them all into a clearing where there are dozens of other evil wizards and witches cheering them. They have joined the new Dark Army!'*

GNASHERS AND THE PACT

Hecate had heard the approach of the old Dark Army. Now she had to assert her authority as joint leader with the Dark Warlord! But it was Cyanor who was leading them forward.

'I have brought back our ancestors as planned. I had to take two hostages to guarantee us safe passage out of the fortress. As long as we keep them alive, we will not be attacked!'

Hecate scanned the evil rabble. 'Where is the Dark Warlord?'

'Lying somewhere else in the fortress. There was no time to find him after the spells were cast. We had to make our escape a priority. They have followed me as their leader ...' Cyanor wanted to remind Hecate of their pact to share power.

But Hecate knew she could control Cyanor and had no intention of sharing power. She had been more concerned about a power struggle with the Dark Warlord. She was secretly pleased he hadn't been revived.

Hecate addressed the newcomers. 'Follow me! We will unite the two Dark Armies now!' She looked at the two hostages. She hated having to keep them alive. But as soon as the combined Dark Army was ready to launch their attack with the zilants, they would be disposed of.

Hecate led them into a clearing where the new Dark Army had assembled. Ugly guttural cheers rang out at the sight of their ancestors. The Deadly Witch raised her voice. 'We must all prepare for battle. Make sure there are enough weapons for everyone. Memorise your evil spells. We launch the attack tonight.'

The Deadly Wizards and Witches stared in pure hatred at Bella and Katy in their golden robes. Their mouths drooled … they would enjoy torturing these two. One of the deadly Wizards came up to Bella and hissed loudly, 'Time someone rearranged your face …'

Hecate saw his evil intentions and shouted, 'NO! They are both to remain alive UNTIL we are ready to fight. Tie them to the tree near Cryptor and Vulpor where my zilant will guard them. Gag them as well.'

Rough hands dragged Bella and Katy out of the clearing and over to the tree where they were gagged and bound. Hecate thought they were best kept out of sight of the Dark Army. She couldn't trust them to obey her orders where Golden Witches were concerned, and they were all terrified of her zilant!

The zilant's eyes flashed angrily as it watched the Deadly Wizards hurry away after binding the hostages to the tree. It came over and sniffed them. Then to Katy's dismay it licked her face with its forked tongue! She could not imagine anything that could look more lethal than the huge fangs protruding from its jaws. Closing her eyes, she bit into her gag. Then she summoned up every ounce of courage and looked directly into the zilant's yellow eyes. Her own eyes expressed kindness and calm. Katy believed in the goodness of creatures. It was only mankind who could turn them into monsters.

The zilant seemed to bore into Katy's very core. It liked what it saw and licked her face again. Its eyes sparkled.

Bella was watching the silent exchange. She knew about zilants from her studies on mystical creatures. *'We are being guarded by a zilant!'* she thought. Then she heard many hisses from the undergrowth behind the zilant. *'There are more of them! Is the Dark Army going to attack the Golden Armies riding on zilants? How on earth have they managed to train these unpredictable creatures?'*

Fango and Dragor were carefully tuning in to Bella and Katy's thoughts from where they had come to a halt on the edge of the thickets. Any closer and they would risk being seen.

'Katy and Bella are tied to a tree. A zilant is guarding them! Bella can hear more zilants! What

are zilants?' Fango asked. He was not at all happy about them being used in an attack.

Danny and Josh knew. They had seen one in a book about powerful creatures. 'A zilant is part snake, part dragon and is winged,' said Danny. He tried to say it in a neutral tone. He didn't want to alarm Ginny with a description of how fearsome a zilant looked. The boys looked at each other. They had promised Lance not to try anything dangerous. And trying to rescue Katy and Bella from under a zilant's nose would be suicidal!

Their thoughts were interrupted by Gnashers. *'Yo' der! So a what-ya-ma-call-it ziiilant has snake blood in it! Could be ma blood brother! De' ziiilants won't suspect a hansom' specimen like me could be a Gold'n Warrrer. I'll mosey in, an' chat wiv de ziiilant. Make us a neeew friend. Read ma mind when I's in der!'*

There was a worried silence as they all tried to grasp what Gnashers intended to do!

'Gnashers! Zilants are huge! And totally unpredictable. You might be killed!' gasped Josh.

'No chance! Us snakes hav' hidd'n charms, only us knows 'bout!'

Without wasting any more time, Gnashers slid quietly into the dense undergrowth. Flicking his tongue out, he found the exact location of the tree Katy and Bella were tied to. *'Found de girls. Dey's tied up but OK,'* he thought.

Then Gnashers saw the zilant. It was bigger than huge! But the zilant was also guarding two shapes on the ground. Gnashers's blood rose! *'Cryptor and de smelly wizzo who let me escape! Man, dis de best news, yet! Dey's gagged and tied up like yella chickins!'*

Gnashers very slowly emerged into the zilant's sight. Time for snake language. *'Yo' der! I's been admirin' yo' fabuuulous fangs! Call me Gnashers, named fo' ma own fangs.'* Gnashers opened his mouth for the zilant to compare.

The zilant eyed him with curiosity. This was the biggest snake it had ever seen, but the zilant wasn't even remotely afraid of Gnashers. In fact, it was bored and tired of guarding captives. This snake might be an interesting diversion. The zilant was secretly impressed that Gnashers wasn't afraid. All other creatures kept well away from zilants!

At that moment, Cryptor spotted Gnashers. He gurgled in fury at the sight of the snake that had terrorised him when he was a rat. But his fury turned to icy fear as Gnashers spread his cobra's hood, eyed him and thought, *'Ma ol' enemy! Read ma mind! I's sooo hungry I could eat a wizzo or two!'*

Vulpor was also staring at Gnashers in horror. The snake was now twice its previous size! With a desperate effort, Vulpor rolled away from Gnashers. Cryptor followed his example. They were both shaking with fear. How was it possible to read the snake's thoughts!

Gnashers was enjoying using his new "wizzo lingo" to strike fear into the evil pair as he allowed them to read his mind. *'Yo' told me to eat brats! Me thinks both o' yo' will do nicely!'*

Gnashers opened his mouth wide and hissed. Cryptor and Vulpor started crying and wetting themselves!

The zilant watched in amazement and then huge amusement. This Gnashers was worthy of being a friend if he could inspire such terror in those evil wizards.

'Call me Devor! I like your style!'

Gnashers bowed his hooded head in a friendly gesture.

The zilant studied Gnashers. *'The evil wizards fear you. Tell me your secret so that I can use it on the evil witch who has me under a spell. Nobody forces zilants to do anything and gets away with it! I can feel her spell wearing off … so tell me your secret before she casts another one. My zilants are waiting for me. We will take our revenge on the evil ones for trying to force us to do their bidding'*

Gnashers could barely contain his excitement. The zilants would turn on the Dark Army as soon as they were able to.

Gnashers went closer to Devor and eyed him. *'Ain't no secret. All spells wear off! Jus' preeetend it ain't worn off in front o' d'eeevil ones an' I'll bring a whole army to help yo' fight dem if yo' let me free dem hostages! Deal?'*

'Deal, Gnashers! Untie them. That young hostage

258

is brave. She's not like those cowards on the floor. She's not afraid of me.'

Gnashers approached the tree. When he located the knots of the ropes binding Bella and Katy, he hooked his fangs into them and pulled them loose taking great care not to release any venom. Gratefully, Katy and Bella pulled the gags out of their mouths as soon as they were freed.

The zilant could feel more control returning to him as the spell weakened further. He went up to Katy and closed his eyes as he very gently nudged her. Katy had that sort of effect on all creatures!

'He likes you, Katy!' whispered Bella.

Katy bravely put out her hand and stroked Devor on his scaly neck. He exhaled with pleasure.

'S'cuse ma buttin' in! Ain't we in de middle o' som' quest fo' revenge?' Gnashers thought.

Devor opened his eyes, *'You can say that again. I am going to get my zilants to circle this camp and attack that miserable excuse of a Dark Army before they can cast more spells.'*

Gnashers now knew for certain the zilants were on their side. *'Giv' us time to get de Gold'n Army here to join de ziiilants an' fix dem eeevil wizzos fo' good! I's one o' de Gold'n Army!'* Gnashers puffed out his hood again.

Devor showed no surprise, *'I thought so. You are some snake, Gnashers! Hurry, before they notice the hostages have escaped'*

Silently, Gnashers led Katy and Bella through

the thicket and back to the group who were anxiously waiting for them. Ginny launched herself at Katy and hugged her tightly. Bella looked at Gnashers and with an emotionally charged voice said, 'Thank you!'

'We have to alert the Golden Army as soon as possible,' Danny said. 'We cannot fly back or we'll be seen by the Dark Army.'

'The village is much closer than the fortress,' Josh said rapidly. 'We can send a message from there! If we head due north we will be somewhere near Owl Lane.'

THE DARK WARLORD

Back at the fortress, Lance was hit by a bombshell when he realised the Dark Army had marched out with a witch leading them. Where was the Dark Warlord? He would never have relinquished control of his evil army if he had been revived! Was this a plot?

'Switch on the security system, Wizzo. Don't let anyone through those gates,' he ordered.

A million scenarios were going through his head as he ran to the keep. The huge door was open, and Fordo was standing there looking distressed. He felt he had failed miserably.

'Did you see the Dark Warlord leave with the others?' Lance asked.

Fordo's eyes opened wide in alarm as he shook his head.

Lance charged into the keep and threw open the door of the chamber where the Dark Warlord had been kept. The chamber was empty!

Nothing made sense! But then, did anything

to do with evil make sense? The most important thing was to check that the schoolchildren were safe. They couldn't afford to have more hostages taken. After that, there would have to be a thorough search of the whole fortress. And at any time, they might have to launch an attack on the Dark Army if Katy and Bella were freed. This was as far from their original plan as it could get.

Down in the shadows of the vault, the Dark Warlord and the wizard who had revived him were waiting for an opportunity to escape. While the noisy rabble had been leaving, it had been possible to locate the Dark Warlord and cast the spell to bring him back without being heard or noticed. By then all the others had left and they were forced to hide.

The Dark Warlord had watched Cyanor leave him in his crystal. His fury when he found out that Cyanor had told *his* army that she did not know his whereabouts knew no bounds. He would hunt her down and take over again!

THE SIGNAL

The Feisty Five, Dragor, Gnashers and Bella had headed north as quickly as they could. Josh was right. They saw houses in the distance and soon reached Owl Lane. They were close to the boys' home. Danny charged into his house to send a message to Wizzo via the disguised phone system.

Back at the fortress, Wizzo was waiting for any news from the androids in the village. When an alert signal flashed, he switched on the camera link. An android was reporting that a group of two dragons and five people had reached Felix and Fabia's house. The android looked at the group and a camera inside one of the android's eyes sent pictures of them with Danny running inside the house.

Even before Danny reached the phone, Wizzo had alerted Lance and Lanzor. Both leaders headed straight to the communications' link just as Danny's call came through.

They listened to Danny's breathless account. Bella and Katy had been rescued and they were all safe. Lance was stunned when he heard there were zilants that would join the Golden Army in battle!

'Brilliant work! Your bravery has given us the chance to win this war! But you must all stay where you are! I will order a full-scale attack from the air now! You will be closest to the combat zone and in possible danger if any of the Dark Army break through. It is too dangerous for you to head back to the fortress in the open. Your dragons will do their best to protect you. Now Lanzor and I must lead the Golden Armies into battle. You will see us pass overhead to the location you have given us. You *must* take cover then!'

But time was running out. The spells cast on Lanzor and his Golden Army and dragons could begin to fade at any time!

THE GOLDEN ARMIES
STRIKE BACK

Lance and Lanzor re-joined the Golden Armies. The armies had been divided into units according to dragon type for several good reasons: the speeds the dragons could achieve, their manoeuvrability in the air, their fire-breathing ability, to name a few.

On hearing the news that the hostages had been saved, they cheered whilst the dragons roared. The battle could now begin! The village had been attacked first and then hostages taken and threatened with death. With the truce well and truly broken, the only course was war.

Lance gave the new Golden Army orders first. 'We are joining forces with zilants that are on the ground circling the Dark Army located in thickets south of Obscura.'

There were astonished gasps at this news. Lance continued, 'The zilants have rebelled against the Dark Army who were trying to force them to be their mounts in battle against us! The zilants are holding off their attack until our arrival!

We will approach at speed from the air and land the first blow on the Dark Army. I will lead the Chameleon Dragon unit in and the Fire Dragon unit is to follow closely. The dragons will rain down fireballs while we unleash our weapons. Meanwhile, the unit of Bird Dragons and Golden Witches are to circle above the battlefield throwing down spells and counter-spells. The Sabre Dragon unit is to fly in after the Fire Dragons. Fly low to allow the dragons to attack with their sabre wings while you use lances.

By this time the zilants will be dealing with any Deadly Wizards and Witches trying to escape. The remaining units of the new Golden Army are to land on the furthest southern edge of the thickets and form a semicircle on the ground behind the zilants.'

Lanzor then gave orders to the old Golden Army. 'As you know, we have limited time before the spells that brought us here lose their power. For this reason, we will fight on the ground. My entire army is to fly and land on Obscura's perimeter road at the north side of the thickets where the Dark Army is located. We will also spread out in a semicircle, following the zilants in. Our aim is to push the Dark Army out of the thickets into the open on the furthest side from the village, where the rest of the new Golden Army will have landed and formed their semicircle. Thus, they will be trapped within a circle of zilants and both our armies!'

Lance turned to Lanzor. 'Whether we win or die in battle, I know in my heart that our fine young wizards and witches will find even stronger spells to bring us back for longer periods. We will meet again, many times. One day we will win the final Wizard War, if not this one.'

Lanzor clasped Lance's hand. 'Let's do our best to win this Great Wizard War.'

The two Golden Warriors soared into the sky as their dragons roared! 'FOLLOW US! SPEED WITH THE WIND!'

Unit by unit the armies followed according to plan.

Back at Felix and Fabia's house, everyone was outside anxiously staring up at the skies. Their family and friends would soon be engaged in a fight for their lives. No outcome was ever assured in war. Time seemed to stand still.

Then they heard the sound of rushing wind, and from high above them, diving down at full speed, came the Chameleon Dragons with Lance at the front. Fango proudly watched his father change into the fiercest Chameleon form.

Danny and Josh saw Felix close behind Lance. Both boys crossed their fingers. *'Please let them win and return safely!'*

The unit of Fire Dragons swooped down after them. Flying high above them were the Golden Witches on Bird Dragons. Ginny and

Katy held their breath as they scanned the unit for Gina and Fabia. They could only hope that all would end well.

There was a louder rush of wind as the Sabre Dragons came in low over the rooftops. The girls could clearly see Tristan on a Sabre Dragon that was related to Dragor. As they flew past, Dragor spread out one of his huge wings to salute them.

In the distance they could hear shouting amid screams and the furious roars of dragons as the battle began! From the same direction, clouds of smoke rose into the sky! The remaining units of the new Golden Army were overhead now and descending on the far side of the battle zone. Then coming in low and fast over their heads came the old Golden Army with Lanzor at its head.

To their amazement they began to land on the road right in front of the house! They watched the seasoned army forming a huge semicircle and start to advance towards the thickets lying beyond the meadows.

Bella took charge of the onlookers. 'We must follow orders and keep out of sight now. If any Deadly Wizards or Witches break through and see us, they may try to take us hostage and tip the balance of war in favour of their side!'

Everyone looked at the two large dragons and wondered how on earth they could be concealed. Casting another invisibility spell on Fango so soon could harm him. An invisibility shield could be walked through …

Danny had an inspiration! 'We'll hide in Cryptor's dungeon! It's easily big enough for all of us. Let's go!'

They went through to Cryptor's garden. The tunnel leading into the dungeon was far too small for both dragons.

'No prob!' Dragor informed them as he displayed the sabres on his wings and set to work widening the tunnel.

As soon as he'd finished, the whole group entered the dungeon. Fango and Gnashers felt chills run down their spines as they recalled the cruelty that Cryptor had shown them there. But these didn't last long, for they realised they were more than a match for Cryptor now.

Bella switched on some dim wall lights. The whole place looked foreboding and eerie, but they were concealed from the outside world. There was an unearthly chill down there. The fire that had once kept Gnashers warm had long died, but there was some firewood next to the hearth.

Danny and Josh stacked some logs in the fireplace and looked at Fango who obliged by lighting it with a fireball. Ginny pointed her wand at the smoke and cast an invisibility spell on it. They had to keep their presence concealed.

The boys went into the chamber where Cryptor kept his instruments of torture. They quickly exited and bolted the door

Fango looked at Dragor. *'We'll take turns to*

stand guard. I'll go first. Gnashers you are able to sleep with your eyes wide open, so you're on watch the whole time!'

While the muffled sounds of war raged on outside, the others sat around the table listening with dread. After a few hours the shouting died down and only occasional yells were heard. Finally, a strange silence descended.

THE END GAME

Hecate and the Dark Army had been taken by complete surprise.

Just as the sun was setting, Hecate had decided it was time to prepare the zilants for battle. Her Dark Army was fully armed and rearing to fight.

She had given her final orders. 'I will lead the zilants into this clearing where we will mount them and fly to the enemy fortress. Their army and dragons will be on the ground. The hostages we took have given us the advantage of attacking first. We will come in low. I'll order the zilants to spray snake venom on the entire Golden Army and their dragons. They will be blinded and helpless while we land and destroy every single one of them. No prisoners are to be taken. Victory will be ours at last!'

Hecate had then gone to get the zilants. Devor watched her approach. He carefully avoided looking into her mesmerising eyes as he waited for her to come within range. The Deadly Witch looked at the tree behind the zilant. Her eyes flashed with fury when she saw the hostages had escaped. Just as she pointed her wand and opened her mouth to scream a death spell at the zilant, Devor opened his mouth and shot a spray of lethal snake venom straight into her face. It coated her eyes and went down her throat. Hecate fell to the ground writhing and gurgling. She was completely helpless. Devor picked Hecate up in his mouth and dragged her deeper into the wood where the other zilants were waiting for him. He dropped the Deadly Witch at their feet.

'That will teach anyone who tries to control a zilant!' he thought. Devor turned to look at the zilants gathering around him. Their eyes shone with fiery anticipation as Devor outlined the plan to surround the Dark Army and wait for the Golden Armies to arrive. The time for revenge had come!

While the zilants were stealthily encircling the Dark Army, the Deadly Wizards and Witches were wondering why Hecate hadn't returned. Maybe she had not been able to control the zilants after all!

Cyanor saw her chance to take over again. Just as she was about to proclaim herself leader, there was a rushing sound overhead! Huge shapes were diving down from the sky unleashing fireballs amidst ferocious roars from

Chameleon Dragons. Spears and spells rained down on them followed by a further storm of fireballs as the next unit of Fire Dragons swooped down!

The Deadly Wizards and Witches were running chaotically in every direction. Their whole camp was burning! They ran shouting and screaming into the thickets, clutching their wands and abandoning their useless weapons. Some of them found themselves cut off by a zilant and were blinded by a spray of snake venom before they could cast a spell! They might have faced a nastier end, but the zilants knew from their foul stench that they were too repulsive to eat! The few who managed to get through the circle of zilants ran into the units of the Golden Armies on the ground.

The Deadly Wizards and Witches were hopelessly outnumbered and were forced to retreat in an ever-tightening circle. Completely surrounded, they dropped their wands and any remaining weapons. Scowling, they reluctantly raised their hands in surrender!

Lance and Lanzor shook hands and embraced while the dragons roared in victory! The second Great Wizard War had been won!

Lanzor addressed the miserable looking rabble. 'Who is your leader? We noticed your Dark Warlord is missing. Will you never learn that war is futile? You broke the truce that was signed after the first Great Wizard War. What reason have we to believe you will sign and honour a peace pact now?'

Cyanor stepped forward. 'I am the new leader. We could not find Mortor,' she lied. 'Soon, we will lose the members of the old Dark Army when the spells that brought them back fade. We have also lost many new fighters in this battle. All we can offer in return for our release is that you keep the bodies of our fallen ones and guard them, as you have done before.'

Lanzor and Lance considered this proposal and then laid down their conditions. 'We will march you to our fortress where a peace pact will be drawn up,' Lance began. 'When you have signed this pact and the spells of life have worn off, those of you left standing will be released. We will indeed keep all your fallen members in high security. But, we *will* ensure that you *never* find them again!'

The valiant leaders signalled the return to the fortress.

Lanzor turned to Lance. 'I am beginning to weaken but I will make it back with Zorgo to carry me. He has more time before his spell wears off.'

'We will never rest until we find stronger spells to bring you both back for longer,' Lance promised. 'We will guard you and protect you with our lives. Evil will never win.'

When they reached the fortress, Lanzor said a fond farewell to Zorgo, 'One day we will meet again and remember this day.'

A peace pact was drawn up for Cyanor to sign. With a sneer returning to her twisted mouth, she scrawled her name on it.

Lance looked at Cyanor and her vile followers. 'We know we cannot trust you. Your numbers are much reduced and you would foolish to attempt another war knowing we have mighty dragons on our side! Nor can you call on zilants to fight for you. They are free to choose sides and they have chosen us in this war! Go back to your swamps and forests or wherever you crawled out of and remain there for eternity. If you ever raise another Dark Army again, I promise you will regret it!'

FINAL JUSTICE

During the battle, nobody had noticed Cryptor and Vulpor lying trussed on the ground in the thicket. The two Deadly Wizards had rolled under bushes and managed to avoid capture. After the wave of zilants and Golden Wizards had passed by, Cryptor had managed to get the gag out of his mouth by hooking it onto a thorny bramble. His face was covered in deep scratches, but at least he had teeth he could use to chew through the whipcord that was binding him. The only problem was he couldn't reach his own bonds. But he could reach Vulpor's …

'Vulpor!' Cryptor hissed. 'I will bite through the whipcord binding you. When you are free, untie me. We have to stick together! The war has been lost by those stupid witches, Hecate and Cyanor. You saw what that zilant did to Hecate. She's finished! But we can still punish Cyanor!'

The need to survive temporarily overrode their hatred for each other. Cryptor rolled towards Vulpor and began to gnaw at the whipcord with his cracked yellow teeth. A nauseating gagging sound erupted from Cryptor as the overpowering reek of dried zilant urine on Vulpor hit his nose. He retched all over Vulpor! Semi-digested dried bats and frogs spewed out of his stomach! They glowered at each other in malign disgust. Each one silently vowed to kill the other after they had hunted down Cyanor!

Cryptor bared his rotten teeth and sank them into the whipcord again. Vulpor couldn't bear to look. If those foul teeth bit into his flesh, he would get gangrene!

At last, Vulpor felt his bonds loosen. He squirmed and contorted until he managed to free his arms and tear the gag out of his mouth. Vulpor was tempted to leave Cryptor there, but his best hope of survival was to stay with Cryptor who knew the area. Reluctantly, Vulpor untied Cryptor.

The two Deadly Wizards staggered to their feet and Cryptor took charge. 'We'll go to the house I used as my base in Obscura. We can lie low and when the coast is clear, we'll call up a couple of warhorses to escape on. But first we need a couple of wands.'

Vulpor loathed taking orders but he couldn't think of a better plan. They searched the battle zone until they found wands that weren't damaged. Then they crept northwards through the thickets and across meadows towards Owl Lane.

Fango was still on guard and Gnashers was at the tunnel entrance when an abominable smell wafted towards them. Gnashers flicked his tongue in out of his mouth and then clamped it shut. *'I smell a dirty rat an' it's headin' dis way wiv an eeeven smellier one!'* he warned. *'It's de two wizzos dat ma zilant pal was guardin'!'*

'It's Cryptor!' thought Fango. *'He must be coming here to hide with another Deadly Wizard. We'll prepare a surprise welcome for them.'* He began to transform into the most ferocious form that only a Chameleon Dragon can achieve.

Gnashers looked at his friend in admiration. *'Man! One look at yo' an' dey'll die o' fright'*

They warned the others of the approaching danger. This was going to be very interesting. Cryptor was about to be confronted by the dragon and snake that he had captured and held in this same dungeon!

'They might use death spells on us!' Katy gasped.

'We will protect you and die in your place if we have to,' Dragor declared. He didn't want to worry them but he was feeling weaker. The spell that brought him to life was wearing off. But he would do all in his power to defend them while he still could.

Bella looked at them as she reassured them. 'We have three wands between us and they will probably have two wands. As we have more magical power, we can deflect their evil spells.

Whatever harm they try inflict on us can be directed back.

'We haven't learnt a deflecting spell yet,' Ginny quickly pointed out.

Bella calmly replied, 'All you need to do is point your three wands as you say "Reversus!" at the same time. They have only seen Gnashers rescue Katy and me, so we will stand looking helpless without wands when they enter. Those evil wizards don't know that Danny, Josh and Ginny were part of the rescue party. So you three should stand hidden behind Fango with your three wands ready to cast the deflecting spell.'

Fango liked the plan. *'They won't be expecting to see me and are likely to try to kill me and Gnashers first. When they begin to raise their wands, I will step aside and you cast your spell. Dragor will wait in the shadows ready to unleash fireballs at them!'*

Ginny ran to turn off the lights. There was just the glow from the fire lighting the dungeon now.

'They will come through the door at the top of those stairs,' Danny said. It was the quickest and easiest way into the dungeon.

They took up their positions facing the door and waited quietly. Danny, Josh, and Ginny stood behind Fango with their wands pointing in the direction of the door. Katy and Bella were in full view of the door. Gnashers was next to Katy and had opened his hood as he raised his head above the ground. He had sacs full of lethal venom to spray at his enemy!

They waited silently. There was the sound of the front door slamming shut and footsteps approaching.

The door to the dungeon was thrown open!

'This is where we'll be safe!' Cryptor snarled as he stepped through the doorway. He froze when he saw the Chameleon Dragon and the massive snake on either side of the two Golden Witches. His face contorted as he noticed that the witches had no wands.

Vulpor was looking at Katy and Bella. 'The hostages!' he muttered.

'Never mind the hostages! Look at those two next to them. Trying to hide in the dark from the big bad wizards are you!' Cryptor snorted. 'My, but you boys have grown up! Methinks it's time to punish you both for escaping!'

Cryptor was under the illusion he could terrify them again while he had the power to cast spells. He was so wrong!

Both Fango and Gnashers knew they could strike maximum fear into those Deadly Wizards! Together they opened their mouths and bared their massive fangs …

Cryptor went pale and stuttered, 'Quick, Vulpor! The Death Spell!'

The two Deadly Wizards were shaking in terror as they raised their wands.

Just before they screeched, 'MORTEM!' Fango stepped aside.

In that same instant Danny, Josh and Ginny shouted, 'REVERSUS!' while pointing their wands.

In perfect timing, Fango and Dragor fired huge fireballs while Gnashers sprayed deadly venom at the two cowardly wizards.

The powerful waves of light surging out of the Deadly Wizards' wands were met halfway by more powerful surges of brilliant light from three wands! A dazzling ball where the two spells met rolled back towards the Deadly Wizards and exploded at the same time that the fireballs and venomous spray hit them. They died on the spot!

As the life faded from Cryptor, he was tortured by the image of the two brats who had ruined his plans.

Everyone silently hoped that Cryptor and Vulpor would never be revived again.

Then the significance of this event hit them! The evil wizard who had started the second Great Wizard War was lying dead at their feet!

FRIENDS FOREVER

A few days later, all the evidence of war had disappeared from Obscura. Everything was returning to normal. School was to resume again, after a holiday to celebrate the victory and to honour all those who had made it possible! Speeches of thanks had been given. The Feisty Five, Gnashers, Dragor and Bella were all awarded golden medals of valour.

The spell to revive the Golden Wizards and Witches of the first Golden Army had worn off. As before, they were lying in their suspended state under the charge of Lance, who had assumed his title of Guardian again. A few members of the new Golden Army who had fallen in battle were beside them. Their fallen dragons were lying close by. It was the intention that they would all be brought back together, when a stronger spell was found.

This time, the fallen Dark Wizards and Witches were hidden in a high security vault in deep underground caves. Only a few knew their location.

Wizzo was fortifying the village and fortress with state of the art surveillance systems. He asked the Feisty Five what would have helped them most when they were tracking the Dark Army.

'Mobile phones!' was the instant reply!

'I thought you'd say that!' he replied as he tossed a mobile phone to each of them. Fango's was super-sized for his large claws. 'You can use yours for texting, Fango!'

Everyone laughed.

Wizzo went on to explain the wizardry behind his new communications system, which now allowed mobile phones to operate. 'I had to design something that could cope with the scrambling signals that keep Obscura safe. By the way, you haven't seen the last of me. I have been asked to give you lot lessons in super modern technology next term!'

Fango and Gnashers thought with relief, *'That's one headache we won't suffer!'*

All too soon, it was time for the dragons to return to their islands and for the zilants to melt away to their secretive places.

Danny, Josh and the girls were sadly preparing to say goodbye to Fango. Felix and Fabia were talking animatedly to Fango's parents and beckoned the Feisty Five to join them.

'We have wonderful news,' said Felix. 'We have asked Fango's family if they would like to live with us. Apparently, the cave behind the waterfall used to be occupied by Fango's ancestors. They have accepted and would like to make the cave their second home.'

The Feisty Five were speechless! Fango began to radiate with happiness. Everyone had tears in their eyes as they hugged Fango.

'Hope those are tears of sympathy for me. I'll have to go to Wizzo's lessons now!' Fango joked.

That left Gnashers.

Ginny looked at him and pleaded. 'Gnashers, I've spoken to Dad, and if you would like to stay with us, Dad will build you the most amazing jungle hangout next to our aquarium.'

Gnashers looked at the Feisty Five. *'Man, I's had de time o' ma life here. But a beeeautiful girl snake has been waitin' fo' me back home. If she's willin' to com' here an' live in wizzo land, pleeeze make de jungle hangout extra big! Fo' when we've got lots o' little wrigglers. But I ain't goin' to Wizzo's lessons!'*

'We'll all go with you to find your girlfriend, Gnashers. And bring you both back!' said Katy.

'Man, I'm gonna tell ma pals all de stories 'bout de Wizzos' War. Impress ma girl, too!'

'When we reach your jungle, Gnashers, I hope your girlfriend isn't hungry!' Josh said with a wicked grin.

Danny whispered to the other members of the Feisty Five, 'Do you think *any* friends of Gnashers will believe his stories?'

'Not a chance!' they chorused!

EPILOGUE

The Guardian never found out what had happened to the Dark Warlord. He was not amongst the evil ones lying in the new vaults, and he hadn't been with the Dark Army when they surrendered. The search for him in the fortress had been interrupted by the battle. There was no trace of Mortor when they had been able to resume looking for him.

Only one searcher harboured the secret of his whereabouts. He had found Mortor and the evil ancestor, who had revived Mortor, hiding in the depths of the keep. Mortor had sensed this Golden Wizard had the potential to be evil, so Mortor promised him that he would share power with him if he changed sides and helped Mortor to escape.

The Dark Warlord's revival was far too late to change the course of the war. The only choice he had was to retreat to safety. Mortor had no intention of being found by the Guardian when the spell of life faded from him. He was already planning a very different future. A future when he would be revived for longer …

Mortor gave the traitorous wizard strict instructions. He was to return to Obscura and resume his previous role and spy as they searched for a more powerful spell of life. The final instruction was chilling … somewhere deep in a forest, the traitor was to dig two shallow graves and set headstones on them so that Mortor could be found again.

Today, there are two headstones in Kielder Forest. One has the inscription, HERE LIES MORTOR. The second simply states, WE WILL RETURN!